A HEART OF DARKNESS

GORDON WALLIS

TABLE OF CONTENTS

Chapter One: London, VICTORIA Train Station, December 5th, Present Day. 1

Chapter Two: Finsbury Park London, Three Days Earlier. 5

Chapter Three: Dilemma 21

Chapter Four: Sharon Pennington 28

Chapter Five: Special Delivery 33

Chapter Six: Zain Usmani 36

Chapter Seven: Appointment 39

Chapter Eight: Puzzles 46

Chapter Nine: Lab Rat 51

Chapter Ten: Ali Usmani 54

Chapter Eleven: South London 56

Chapter Twelve: Ali Usmani 60

Chapter Thirteen: Spy Cam 64

Chapter Fourteen: Arrears 73

Chapter Fifteen: Appointment 76

Chapter Sixteen: Rashid Abdulrahman 79

Chapter Seventeen: Paranoia 85

Chapter Eighteen: Brandon Stevens 88

Chapter Nineteen: South London 91

Chapter Twenty: Zain Usmani 98

Chapter Twenty One: Brandon Stevens 101

Chapter Twenty Two: Green 105

Chapter Twenty Three: Zain Usmani 108

Chapter Twenty Four: Confrontation 111

Chapter Twenty Five: Zain Usmani 116

Chapter Twenty Six: Confessions 119

Chapter Twenty Seven: The Missing 122

Chapter Twenty Eight: Bang 125

Chapter Twenty Nine: Akim Usmani 128

Chapter Thirty: Green 132

Chapter Thirty One: Akim Usmani 136

Chapter Thirty Two: Vertigo 143

Chapter Thirty Three: Usmani 147

Chapter Thirty Four: Green.. 152

Chapter Thirty Five: Usmani 156

Chapter Thirty Six: Green.. 159

Chapter Thirty Seven: Usmani... 167

Chapter Thirty Eight: Green 174

Chapter Thirty Nine: Usmani... 194

Chapter Forty: Green 201

Chapter Forty One: Usmani 205

Chapter Forty Two: Green 208

Chapter Forty Three: Usmani 211

Chapter Forty Four: Green... 215

Chapter Forty Five: Potters Bar, London, 10 days later 227

CHAPTER ONE

London, VICTORIA Train Station, December 5th, Present Day.

Thirty five year old Zain Usmani shivered involuntarily as he walked out of the warm fug of the underground and into the icy air of the busy Victoria Station concourse above. Around him swarmed a sea of humanity all making their way hurriedly to their various platforms and destinations. Following the route he had planned so meticulously, he made his way through the crowds towards the escalators that led to the upper shopping level that faced the departure boards. Despite the freezing temperatures, Zain Usmani was sweating profusely and he pulled the blue hoodie lower around his face in an effort to shield himself from the many surveillance cameras. His jaw moved constantly as he nervously chewed the large lump of gum in his mouth. He glanced at his cheap digital watch as he approached the escalators. His eyes strained as he battled to read the time through the thick nonprescription reading glasses he had purchased in Finsbury Park only hours before. The glasses were an attempt at hiding his natural features as was the fact that he wore bright trendy clothing as opposed to his traditional dark grey tunic and Muslim skull cap. The time was 8.35 pm and the station was bursting at the seams with peak traffic after a day's work in the city. At the base of the escalators to the left hand side, a group of young school children stood in a group singing Christmas carols. A number of people milled around them smiling and taking pictures with their phones as they sang. This unexpected obstacle irritated Zain Usmani and he grunted in annoyance as he made his way around the crowd. On his back he wore a fake Adidas rucksack but despite the thick jacket he wore, the weight of it caused the shoulder straps to cut painfully into his thin shoulders. The rucksack he carried contained a 6kg low pressure gas cylinder filled with a mixture of ammonium nitrate powder and diesel. Packed tightly around the cylinder were numerous plastic bags of steel bolts and nails. Zain Usmani was carrying a crude but deadly homemade bomb. With his head still hung low he stepped onto the escalator and steadied himself by gripping the moving black hand rail with his left hand.

"Allahu Akbar" he whispered to himself as he wiped the sweat from his forehead with his right hand.

Zain Usmani lifted his gaze briefly as the escalator reached the top and he stepped off. Through the blur of the glasses he saw that the Weatherspoons pub was full of punters as expected. A sudden wave of fear rushed over him and once again he wiped the sweat from his forehead whilst blinking rapidly.

"Alhamdulillah.." he whispered to himself. *All praise is due to God alone.*

With his head hung low once again he walked towards the packed entrance to the pub. The slight limp in his gait was due to the mild palsy he had suffered from oxygen starvation during complications at childbirth. Zain Usmani also suffered from learning difficulties and various other cognitive and behavioral issues. His taller and more handsome twin brother, Ali, had been spared this problem causing Zain to be regarded as the quiet or weak brother in the family. Zain Usmani had always seen this as a curse. Some cruel and unusual punishment unfairly inflicted on him by the infidels of the world. But today, he intended to right some of those wrongs once and for all. The tables to his right near the balcony were packed with groups of office workers while the small entrance to the pub was crowded with a group of the same. Loud raucous laughter seemed to engulf him as he approached and this only added to his sense of fear and trepidation. It was only as he shuffled through the glass doors at the entrance of the pub that he saw a small space to his left that would suit. The nearby table was full and the seated patrons were busy placing their drink orders with a colleague who was battling to remember their requests. Zain Usmani quickly took the bag from his shoulders and opened it whilst holding it to his chest. He stared down at the simple mechanical oven timer he had attached to the 12 volt lead acid battery. With a quick movement he turned the switch on the timer to the 10 minute mark. The noise in the long room masked the clicking sound it produced as he did so.

The sweat on Zain Usmani's face caused the glasses to slip down his nose and he hurriedly pushed them back up before closing the rucksack once again. At the far side of the room he saw the large oak barrel that had been converted into a table. There were a number of bags around the foot of it that had been placed there by the occupants of a nearby cubicle. He had identified this table as a suitable spot to place his deadly package on a previous visit.

On his right, the bar was crowded as the staff battled to keep up with the barrage of orders from the thirsty punters. Zain Usmani made his way slowly through the room between the tables to his left and the crowds at the bar to his right. His mind was spinning and the noise in the room seemed to grow louder in his ears as he walked. As he reached the barrel table at the end of the room he carefully placed his heavy bag near the others on the floor and stepped through the glass doors at the rear into the fresh air outside. Without looking back he turned right and walked towards the open thoroughfare that led around the small pub. There was a brief respite from the crowds as he made his way around the side of the building until once again he found himself at the entrance. As he walked past he attempted to take one last look at the bag but his view was blocked by a group of men in dark suits standing in his line of sight. Without pausing, Zain Usmani made his way to the escalators and began his descent to ground level. The shrill voices of the carol singing children seemed louder now and he felt a desperate urge to get away. Still sweating and chewing furiously he made his way towards the front of the grand old building. The night was cold and dark and the lights on the streets outside were blurred through the cheap reading glasses. Zain Usmani pulled them from his face and turned left heading towards Elbury Street.

"Allahu Akbar" he muttered to himself repeatedly as he walked.

It was five minutes later when Zain Usmani finally stopped walking and stood in the light of a nearby Bureau De Change. His left wrist trembled as he checked the time on his watch.

"Yeah..." he muttered to himself "Tonight we will see what the runt of the litter can do."

CHAPTER TWO

Finsbury Park London, Three Days Earlier.

"What can you see Jason? What's going on?" said Brandon Stevens in his broad cockney accent.

"You need to learn to be patient, Brandon.." I said as I peered through the binoculars "Especially in this job."

I took the small pair of binoculars from my eyes and turned to look at the young man who sat opposite me in the passenger seat of the hired vehicle. His gaudy pin striped suit was ruffled and his green eyes were bright and alert in his ruddy face. His unruly blonde hair was styled to the latest trend. At only 24 years old he had been assigned as an intern by the insurance company to assist me on this particular case. Although he was a thoroughly likeable young fellow, his enthusiasm and bluster was starting to become tedious. I glanced at the street to my right and noticed the coffee shop had begun to fill up with the late afternoon trade. I reached into my pocket and pulled out a £20 note.

"Why don't you go and grab us some food?" I said handing him the note "Get some coffee as well."

"Yeah of course" he said as he took the note "What would you like Jason?"

"I'll leave it up to you.." I said as he got out of the vehicle.

There was a sudden blast of cold air and I watched as the young man crossed the road in the light drizzle that blew in from the shroud of grey sky above. Lifting the binoculars to my eyes once again I focussed on the front door of the subject of the investigation, 56 year old Akim Usmani. A Pakistani national, he ran a successful small business importing ceramic tiles and leather goods from his home country along with regular shipments of coffee from Kenya. It had been three months since his firm had filed its claim with the insurance company and the issue was yet to be resolved.

An assessor had been sent to his South London warehouse to inspect a shipment of decorative tiles said to have been damaged during transit. The claim had been to the tune of £40,000.00 but the assessor had been met by uncooperative staff at the warehouse and had been unable to correctly quantify the damaged stock. In his opinion, the value of the damaged goods he had seen was roughly £15,000.00 and when asked where the remainder of the damaged tiles were, he had been told they had been erroneously removed by a waste disposal service. The insurance company had decided that things weren't adding up and had escalated the case by asking me to take a look at Mr Usmani and his business dealings. Young Brandon Stevens had arrived on my doorstep the previous morning and we had spent the afternoon watching Usmani's address from the same very spot. I had been given a file with very little information apart from the fact that he ran the business with his twin sons, Ali and Zain. The family, being devout Muslims, were said to be quiet, deeply religious, and actively involved in the day to day running of the nearby Finsbury Park Mosque. This had appeared to be accurate save for one of the twins, Ali, who I had photographed the previous day racing up the street in a silver BMW whilst playing loud rap music. A good looking young man who dressed in flashy, expensive clothes, he appeared to be the opposite of his brother Zain who I had also photographed visiting the Mosque with his father the previous day. Both Zain and his father wore the standard dark grey tunics and white skull caps of their faith. Shorter and with a somewhat hunched back, Zain walked with a slight limp never looking up from his path. Although I could not tell for sure, it had appeared to me at the time that he might be slightly retarded. I opened the thin file that lay in the centre console of the vehicle and looked at the three printed photographs of the men. All wore beards in keeping with their faith although Ali's beard was meticulously trimmed and neat. The father of the family, Akim, was a big man. His long beard was streaked with thick lines of grey hair. All of the men had large hooked noses which gave them a noble appearance save for Zain who appeared slightly mousey and dishevelled. I sighed and turned the heating up as I replaced the photographs in the file. I looked down the street towards the front door of the Usmani household.

The door remained closed and there was no movement. At that moment Brandon returned carrying a couple of rolls and a tray with two cups of coffee. His unruly blonde hair was damp with tiny droplets of rain. I leant over to open the door for him and he climbed in beside me.

"Ham and salad roll and a filter coffee.." he said.

"Perfect."

It was five minutes later when I saw the door of the modest double storey detached house open. I lifted the binoculars to see one of the twins, Ali, step out and walk towards the parked silver BMW nearby.

He wore a dark blue shell suit with expensive looking trainers and I noticed a heavy gold chain around his left wrist.

"Well now, looks like he's going for another drive" I said to Brandon handing him my cup "Let's follow him.."

The sudden break from the monotony of the day lifted his spirits and he took the paper cup from me with wide eyes. I started the engine and prepared to do a U-turn as I watched the young man climb into his vehicle. As he had done the day before, Ali Usmani drove past us at speed with loud music playing. I drove out of the parking bay and turned the small vehicle around as fast as possible. The traffic at the top of the road was busy enough to slow Ali down and I soon caught up with him at the intersection. I thought initially that he might be heading to the nearby Mosque which was a few hundred metres to the right, but this was proved wrong when he headed straight past the Finsbury Park tube station and took the main road up towards Highbury and Islington. The young man drove aggressively and for a minute I lost him until he got caught behind a bus and I was able to catch up. The rain began to fall heavily as we reached the top of the hill just past the turn off to the Emirates football stadium. I slowed the vehicle as I noticed Ali indicating he was about to make a left turn into an alleyway in between some shops. Seeing a space on the opposite side of the road I pulled across and parked outside a pub called The Queen's Head.

Ali Usmani had parked in the alleyway near some rubbish bins and was hurriedly making his way back to the street through the rain. When he arrived he immediately turned left and ducked under the awning of a kebab shop. The takeaway was situated in an old two storey building with a convenience store next door. In between the two shops was a single yellow door that obviously led to the flat upstairs. There was a large red sign above the entrance to the takeaway that read 'Supreme Kebabs'. The front windows of the establishment were slightly misted up from the heat of the interior so I lifted the binoculars to my eyes for a closer look. Ali Usmani was nowhere to be seen.

"He must have gone around the back of the shop" I muttered to Brandon "I can't see him."

"You want me to go take a look, Jason?" he replied.

"Why not?" I said still peering through the binoculars "I think go in there like a customer, place an order, and while you're waiting for it, take a look at the food hygiene certificate. I can see a notice board on the left wall near the till. The certificate should be there. All food outlets are required to have them by law. The owner's name will be on that certificate. See whose name is on it."

I turned to look at Brandon who was clearly excited at the prospect of actually doing something other than sitting in a parked vehicle for hours on end.

"Act casual, Brandon" I said with a half smile "Like just any another customer.."

"Yeah of course" he said with wide eyes "Will do.."

I watched as the young man climbed out of the car and dashed across the street through the rain into the shelter of the shop. I lifted the binoculars once again to take a look but there was no sign of Ali. *Where did he go?* The rain pattered on the windscreen and the wet pavement outside the pub glistened black in the pale late afternoon light.

I glanced at my watch as I waited and saw it had just gone 3.20 pm. The yellow glow of the lights in the pub was warm and inviting and I wished that I was in there rather than the frigid hired car. Five minutes later Brandon emerged and ran back across the street carrying a takeaway box. He opened the passenger door and climbed in hurriedly.

"The name on the certificate is A. Usmani, Jason" he said placing the box in the foot well "It must be Ali's shop."

"Could be his father, Akim" I replied "Either way this is good information. Looks like he'll be in there for a while, I think we'll go back to the house for now."

The mid afternoon traffic was heavy and it took a few minutes to leave the parking spot. I took a right down a service lane for The Queen's Head pub and reversed back onto the road. It was 3.55 pm and the sky was darkening by the time I pulled into my regular spot near the Usmani house. I could tell that Brandon was disappointed to return to the monotony of the surveillance after the brief activity of the day.

"We'll leave at 5.00 pm if nothing else happens here" I said to appease him.

It was at exactly 4.00 pm when the front door of the house opened and two men stepped out. Taking advantage of a lull in the rain, Akim Usmani and his son, Zain stepped out and began walking towards us on the opposite side of the road.

"Going to the Mosque again?" said Brandon quietly.

"Maybe..." I said "We'll follow them."

Akim Usmani was a big man and he walked with confidence while his much smaller son, Zain, limped along behind him with his head bowed. Brandon and I sat in silence as they passed us on the opposite side of the road heading towards the junction.

I waited until they had walked a good thirty metres past us before starting the engine and doing a U-turn. The street was fairly busy but it was easy enough to crawl along behind the two men without losing them. Soon enough they reached the junction and both men turned right.

"I think you're right Brandon" I said "Looks like they're headed to the Mosque, just like yesterday."

The junction was crammed with traffic and I was unsure if I would find a parking spot near the Mosque.

"Why don't you follow them on foot?" I said "There's too much traffic."

"Sure, no problem. Where will I meet you?" he asked, raring to go.

"I'll be back at the usual spot" I said "Just keep an eye on them from the other side of the road.."

"Will do, cheers!" he said as he got out out of the car.

I watched as the young man crossed the street and made his way to the right towards the Mosque. Smoking was prohibited in the hired car and I needed one desperately so I made a quick U-turn and headed back to my parking spot near the Usmani house. The sky was darkening rapidly and the street lights above came on as I opened the door and stepped out into the frigid, damp air to smoke. I pulled my jacket tighter around my body and leant back on the vehicle as I lit up. The routines of the men had seemed fairly standard so far and the only new information had been the fact that the kebab shop was owned by them. *You're gonna have to go down to South London tomorrow and take a look at their warehouse. No point doing the same thing again and again here in Finsbury Park, Green. Plus, it's killing young Brandon.* The wet street glistened and tendrils of smoke curled upwards in the yellow glow of the street light above me as I exhaled.

"Oh yes....." I said to myself quietly "Another day, another dollar."

It was 4.45 pm when I saw Akim and Zain Usmani returning home in the rear view mirror of the vehicle. Once again Zain lagged behind his father who walked swiftly down the pavement. I watched both men intently as they passed on the far side of the street. The father, Akim, was a big man with a strong jawline beneath his bushy beard. The smaller, hunched figure of his son, Zain, followed as usual from behind. A minute later the passenger door opened and a shivering Brandon climbed in.

"Was just like you said, Jason" he said closing the door "They went to the Mosque, did their thing, and came straight back.."

"Okay.." I replied "Well that's fine. I think tomorrow we'll go and take a look at their warehouse in South London. Hopefully we'll learn a bit more and it won't be as boring for you."

"No it's all good..." he said with a smile "I'm here to learn."

"Okay" I said starting the engine "Well, I think we'll head off now. It's been a long day. I'll head home, you can take the car and pick me up in the morning."

"Yeah sure, Jason. Can do..."

It took some time to make it past the busy junction and the traffic crawled up the hill towards Highbury and Islington. It was as we passed the turn off to the Emirates stadium that I began thinking of the other son Ali, and the kebab shop. *It warrants further scrutiny Green, it's not far from home and there's a pub opposite too.*

"On second thoughts, Brandon" I said "I think I'll go and have some dinner at that pub across the road from the kebab shop. I can get a cab home later and at the same time I can keep an eye on the place. I'll stop there and you carry on home."

"You sure Jason?" he replied "I can join you..."

"Nah, It's no bother mate" I said as we approached the top of the hill "I'll only be a couple of hours. Don't expect to see much anyway.."

With the rain still holding off I pulled over near a bus stop just before the take away and engaged the hand brake. We both got out of the vehicle together and after saying our goodbyes I began walking up the pavement towards the shop. The sky was totally dark above and the wet tarmac glimmered in the yellow glow from the street lights above. Ali Usmani's BMW was still parked in the dark alleyway when I reached the front of the takeaway but when I glanced inside he was still nowhere to be seen. The traffic on the road was heavy and I had to stand back from the tarmac to avoid being splashed by the cars. The rain returned as I dashed across the road during a break in the traffic and I shivered as I reached the awning in front of the pub. The need to get warm was greater than my craving for a cigarette so I pushed the brass handle of the heavy door and stepped inside. The interior was richly decorated, warm and soundproofed from the noise of the traffic outside. I walked up to the bar to find a portly bald man stacking glasses on shelves. He turned to me with raised eyebrows as I walked up.

"Evening" he said in a cockney accent "What can I get you?"

"I'll have a pint of Lowenbrau please.."

I turned to look at the windows as the man pulled the pint. There was long bench table with pine stools along the front with a clear view across the road to Supreme Kebabs. *That'll do fine*. I paid for the beer, took a menu from the counter, and walked over to the front windows to choose my seat. The beer was cold and crisp and I drank it slowly as I idly stared across towards the front of the kebab shop and the BMW of Ali Usmani parked in the dark alleyway. The street and pavements shimmered yellow and silver in the glow of the constant stream of vehicle lights and pedestrians rushed past huddled under their umbrellas. It was some twenty minutes later that the need to smoke outweighed my desire to stay indoors in the warmth. I nodded to the barman as I walked to the door and stepped outside into the frigid air under the awning.

It was as I lit the cigarette that I noticed the girl walking up the street on the opposite side of the road. Wearing tight white leggings and a puffy pink jacket, she made her way quickly up the street and stopped near the yellow door between the kebab shop and the convenience store. I'm not sure what it was about her that attracted my attention, but for some reason she appeared uneasy and frustrated. I watched as she pulled a pack of cigarettes from her cheap white handbag and lit one. Youthfully plump, with her long blonde hair pulled into a pony tail atop her head, she couldn't have been more than 15 or 16 years old. I pulled my jacket tighter around me and leant back against a pillar in the wall as I watched her. Her impatience seemed to grow more and more acute with every passing minute and I noticed her repeatedly scratching her arms. *Strange*. It was as I crushed out my own cigarette on the pillar and stepped forward to throw the butt into a bin that I saw her take a phone from her bag. Clearly frustrated, she dialled a number and stood waiting for whoever she was calling to answer. It was as I was about to turn around and head back into the warmth of the pub that I saw her gesticulating with her left hand as she spoke. At that moment I saw the tall figure of Ali Usmani step out from the back area of the takeaway opposite and make his way towards the entrance. He walked swiftly out of the door and turned left to face the girl who stood in her spot near the yellow door between the shops. It was clear she had been on the phone to him and had been complaining about something as I could see heated words exchanged between the two of them. I stepped back into the shadow and shelter of the awning to continue watching. A few seconds later Ali Usmani pulled a set of keys from his pocket and opened the yellow door between the shops. There was a further exchange of words between the two then the girl stepped inside and closed the door behind her. With the girl gone, Ali Usmani looked around the street furtively, made his way back into the takeaway, and disappeared into the back area once again. It was a few seconds later that I saw the lights in the flat above the kebab shop come on. By then my own hands were aching with the cold so I walked back into the snug interior of the pub. It had been an unusual exchange between the girl and Ali and it stayed in my mind as I walked up to the bar.

"Same again?" asked the portly barman.

"Sure, thanks.."

I glanced towards the window once again as the man pulled the pint and wondered what the conversation had been about. *Could be simply the Usmani's own the building and she is a tenant in the flat upstairs. But she's too young for that. Who knows?* I walked back to my seat at the window and browsed the menu I had collected earlier. The shepherd's pie stood out from the rest of the fare so I walked back and placed my order with the barman. It was when I returned to my seat that I saw the first man arrive at the yellow door across the road. Clearly of the Muslim faith, he wore a long beard and I put his age at roughly 45 years old. He pulled a set of keys from a pocket under his tunic before opening the door and stepping inside. A frown formed on my forehead as I drank the beer and watched. *This is strange, Green.* Although the upstairs light was on above the kebab shop, the curtains were drawn and I could see no movement beyond them. It was some twenty minutes later, as I was eating my dinner, that the door opened and the man emerged onto the street. He ambled off casually down the pavement into the darkness and disappeared. The food was good and I carried on eating and sipping my beer as I watched. The second man arrived exactly ten minutes later and he too pulled a key from his pocket and entered the door. Although he wasn't dressed in traditional Muslim garb, he wore a beard with a skull cap on his fat bald head. *This is very strange indeed.* As the previous man had done, the fat man emerged some 30 minutes later and walked back in the direction he had come from. The lights in the upstairs flat remained on and there was no sign of the girl. I drummed my fingers on the surface of the table as I watched and waited. The third man to arrive was none other than Akim Usmani himself. Driving a dark coloured Volvo station wagon, he parked behind the BMW of his son in the alley way to the left of the shop. There was no mistaking his tall heavy frame and grey streaked beard. He stopped briefly in the doorway of the kebab shop and exchanged some words with the staff before he too walked over the to the yellow door and entered. *What the fuck is going on here?* There had been a steady stream of men all visiting the flat upstairs and the young girl I knew to be up there.

This is starting to look pretty sinister, Green. Of course, I had read about the phenomenon of grooming gangs in the North of the country and there had been some reports of this going on in London as well. I turned and nodded at the barman as he finished with another customer and he acknowledged my order for another drink. Akim Usmani emerged from the door an hour later and left in the Volvo without stopping at the takeaway. I glanced at my watch to see it was approaching 9.45 pm. The small crowds of punters in the pub were beginning to thin out as were the customers for the kebab shop across the road. It was 15 minutes later while I was standing outside for a cigarette that the last man arrived. He came on a moped which he parked on the pavement nearby and let himself into the door. The man had no beard but was clearly of Asian descent and once again I watched for any movement from behind the curtains. There was none. It was 10.30 pm when the barman finally called time and the last of the punters began making their way home. I finished the dregs of my pint and waved at the barman who was busy cashing up behind the till. The air outside was bitingly cold but I stood at the pillar and lit a cigarette as I waited to see what would happen next. The staff in the kebab shop were busy cleaning the front of the establishment in preparation to close as well, but the last man remained upstairs with girl. It was a full 15 minutes later when he emerged, quickly donned his crash helmet, and left on the moped. By then I was freezing and most of the staff at the kebab shop had left leaving only Ali who was still out of sight behind the scenes. *Just wait for him to leave, Green. He can't stay there all night.* Suddenly the upstairs light went out and I wondered for a few seconds if the girl had gone to sleep. I was proved wrong when I saw the yellow door open and the girl step out onto the street. She stood there in the cold near the door and pulled a small make up compact from her handbag. She flicked it open and tended to her heavy make up in the reflection of the tiny mirror. When she was done she replaced the compact and stood there waiting. Once again she appeared frustrated and impatient and she scratched at her arms through her thick pink jacket as she stood there. *She's waiting for him as well.* My suspicions were proved correct when I saw her repeatedly turn to look through the darkened windows of the kebab shop. It was five minutes later when Ali Usmani finally stepped out into the shop front and walked towards the doors.

He walked outside, glancing quickly at the young girl, and then turned to lock the doors with a set of keys. The street was a lot quieter than it had been earlier so I backed up into a darker area near the pillar to avoid being seen. After locking the door to the shop, Ali walked up to where the girl waited and a few words were exchanged. Once again the girl appeared somehow upset or frustrated and appeared to be almost begging the young man for something. I pulled my phone from my pocket and began taking video footage as the conversation continued. Although the two were at some distance, I was able to zoom in enough to get a clear but slightly shaky picture. Ali Usmani looked around briefly then reached into a pocket and pulled a tiny plastic bag which he handed to the girl. The girl almost snatched it from him, spun around on her heels, and walked off in a hurry. *Drugs. Has to be.* I continued taking video as Ali turned around and walked in the opposite direction towards the alley way on the left. I watched as he unlocked the BMW, climbed in, and reversed slowly onto the street. He paused briefly for a night bus that was passing then swung around and headed off in the direction of the family house. *Well, well. It seems there is lot more going on here than simple insurance fraud. A lot more.* I watched as the rear lights of the vehicle disappeared over the hill and then took a look at the shop once again. All of the lights were out in the upstairs rooms and both the convenience store and kebab shop were closed. I decided to take advantage of the fact that the streets were pretty much empty and take a closer look at the building. Shivering from the cold, I stepped out of the darkness under the awning and crossed the wet street. I tried briefly to take a peek through the window behind the counter on the takeaway but my line of sight was blocked by a partition wall. Instead I walked off to the left and stepped into the alleyway where Ali and his father had parked their vehicles. The surface was cobbled and slippery underfoot and the two large rubbish bins smelt of rotten food waste. The building was an old Georgian detached house that had been converted into shops many years beforehand and there was a small area to the rear that had been fenced off with a low wooden wall. It took some time for my eyes to adjust to the darkness but soon enough I saw the simple latch and lock for the gate. I looked up at the second floor of the building and immediately saw there were no lights on in the old sash windows. *There's no-one up there Green. Looks like it's a flat that's being used for one purpose and one purpose only.*

Running up the centre of the back wall was a heavy old drain pipe. I knew it would be easy to scale and the old sash windows were simple to open from the outside. *But this is outside your brief, Green. This is not why you are here.* After a final look at the windows I walked back up the dark alleyway and back onto the street. I summoned a nearby Uber cab from my phone and stood under a street light smoking a cigarette as I waited. The ride back to my flat in Seven Sisters only took

10 minutes at that late hour and it was with great relief that I finally stepped into the warmth of the living room and headed to the bathroom for a shower. As the steaming water ran over my body I stood with my eyes closed and leant against the tiles. When I was done, I dried myself off and lay on my bed to think about the strange turn of events the evening had brought. *Whatever was actually going on in that flat is not in your brief, Green. You are supposed to be looking at the business activities of Mr Akim Usmani. That's all.* I grappled with these thoughts for the next few minutes until I began to drift off to sleep. The last thing I remember was the vision of the young blonde girl standing near the yellow door. Standing there looking desperate and scratching at her arms. Then there was darkness.

CHAPTER THREE

Dilemma

I awoke at 6.30 am with a dry mouth from the beer and reached for the glass of water on the bedside. Lying back with my hands behind my head I stared at the ceiling and went through the events of the previous evening in my mind. The dilemma I faced was fairly simple but difficult to deal with at the same time. Apart from the fact that I had no idea what had actually transpired in the flat above the kebab shop, there was also the possibility that the girl was actually above the age of consent. Then there was the fact that what I had witnessed was really nothing to do with my professional brief in as far as the business activities of the Usmani's were concerned. These thoughts continued to swim around my mind as I got up and boiled the kettle for coffee. I walked across the lounge with coffee mug in hand and pulled the curtains of the bay window open. The frozen urban landscape below was soaked and shrouded in a light mist that clung to the streets like moss. I sighed deeply and sipped from the steaming mug as I stared out at the bleak, darkened vista below. I walked to the table where my phone lay on charge and watched the video I had taken of the exchange between the girl and Ali. Although there was no way to prove it, I had very little doubt in my mind that the tiny plastic bag had contained drugs of some sort. *It would explain her agitated state, Green. It has to be drugs*. After finishing the coffee I went for a shower and shave then got dressed for the day. I had decided that I would tell young Brandon about what I had witnessed and show him the video as well. I was certain that he would come to the same conclusion that I had. The early news on the television was drowned out by the sizzle of bacon and sausages as I cooked a breakfast. Brandon Stevens rang the door intercom at exactly 8.00 am as expected and I told him to come up to the flat. His face was flushed with cold as I greeted him, let him into the flat and offered him a seat.

"Well.." I said "There were some pretty strange things going on at the kebab shop last night."

The young man sat forward in his seat and listened intently to my detailed account. I went on to tell him of the exchange at the end of the night and showed him the video I had taken.

"Ah, there's no doubt" he said sitting back "That's gear for sure.."

"So.." I said "We have a problem now. If this girl is under age like I suspect, we would be morally compelled to report this to the police. The drugs would be secondary in that case."

"What we gonna do, Jason?"

"Well, I think we shelve going to the warehouse for now and head back to the house and the kebab shop. We take pictures and try to learn some more."

"Sounds good to me.."

The interior of the hired car was freezing and I ran the engine for a few minutes as I waited for the heating to kick in. The main road to

Highbury and Islington was busy and a light patter of rain fell as we passed the kebab shop on the right. In the cold light of day the exterior of the building looked shabby and dirty and we both stared at it as we passed. It took a further 20 minutes to get to Finsbury Park and arrive at the familiar parking spot near the Usmani house. It was a full hour later when I got out of the vehicle for a cigarette and then walked across the road to the cafe to get some coffee.

"We'll give it another half hour here, if nothing happens we'll head back up to the kebab shop" I said as I handed Brandon his cup.

"Sweet.." said Brandon.

As I had expected, there was no movement from the Usmani household and the front door remained firmly closed. To break the boredom I sent young Brandon walking down the opposite side of the road telling him to take a few clandestine pictures of the house as he passed. I used the opportunity to smoke a cigarette and stood huddled into my jacket near the car as I did so.

He returned a few minutes later and we both studied the pictures on his phone.

"Well" I said "There's nothing unusual there..."

"No" he replied "Pretty much like any other house on the street."

"Exactly. I think we'll head back up to the kebab shop and see what gives.."

The drive back up the hill was relatively easy in the mid morning traffic and the very same parking spot I had used the previous day was free. Although the convenience store next door was open, the doors of the kebab shop were still closed. I glanced at my watch to see it had just gone 10.45 am.

"They'll be opening soon I'm sure" I said "Getting ready for the lunch time trade."

Fifteen minutes later, as if on cue, two young Asian men arrived and opened the shop. They busied themselves in the shop front cleaning and switching on the illuminated menu boards as they prepared for the day's trade. Brandon and I sat watching in silence until a number 19 bus headed to Finsbury park stopped in the traffic next to us and blocked our vision. It came as a surprise to suddenly see the young girl from the previous evening step off the bus not 5 metres from where we sat. She carried what looked like an empty sports bag as well as her usual handbag.

"That's her" I said quietly as I watched her "That's the girl from last night.."

Brandon remained quiet as he watched her pull her puffy pink jacket tighter around her chubby frame in an effort to stay warm. She wore black tights and her eyes appeared slightly glazed over in her heavily made up face.

"She can't be more than 14 or 15 years old, Jason..." said Brandon as he studied her "And she looks well out of it. High as a kite."

We watched as she stood directly in front of our vehicle and waited for a gap in the traffic. When eventually there was one, the blonde pony tail atop her head bobbed as she trotted across the road towards the kebab shop. Seemingly calmer than she had been the previous night, she leant against the yellow door between the two shops and pulled a packet of cigarettes from her handbag.

"Looks like she's waiting to be let in again..." I said.

"Yeah.." said Brandon as he stared across the road "Early start."

The girl stood leaning against the door as she smoked casually and Brandon took a number of photographs of her. It was exactly 5 minutes later when I saw the familiar Volvo arrive and park in the alleyway near the dumpsters once again.

"Looks like the father Akim is here again.." said Brandon.

We watched as the door of the vehicle opened and a man climbed out.

"That's not Akim" I said as I saw the smaller frame "That's the other son, Zain."

"You're right, it is..."

We watched as Zain limped up the alley way and turned left. Instead of making his way into the kebab shop he walked straight up to the waiting girl and began talking to her.

"Are you getting pictures, Brandon?" I asked as I watched.

"Yep, I am.."

It was then that Zain pulled a piece of paper from under his grey tunic and held it out so the girl could read it. He pointed at the words written on it and mouthed something as if to make a point to the girl. She nodded in understanding, took the paper from him, and placed it in her handbag. Zain then pointed North up the main road with his right hand and began giving the girl what appeared to be directions. Once again she nodded in understanding. Finally he handed her some cash which she took quickly.

"He's sending her somewhere.." I muttered.

"Certainly looks like it."

With the conversation over, Zain nodded at the girl and began walking back to the parked Volvo in the alleyway. The girl slung the empty sports bag over her shoulder and walked over to the shelter of a nearby bus stop. She sat inside and lit another cigarette while she waited. Knowing that Brandon would relish the opportunity to break the monotony of the surveillance, I spoke.

"Why don't you follow her?" I said.

"Yeah?" he replied "Can do.."

"Sure.." I said "Keep your distance, get off the bus wherever she gets off, and see what she's up to. I'll stick around here for now and you can call me if there's anything interesting."

I turned to look at Brandon who by then was wide eyed and itching to leave.

"Keep your distance like I said, Brandon.."

"Will do.." he said as he climbed out of the vehicle.

I watched as he crossed the busy street and made his way towards the bus stop.

When he arrived he glanced at his watch, pulled his phone from pocket, and leant against the shelter casually. Feeling the need for a cigarette I stepped out of the car and walked over to the pillar where I had stood the previous night to smoke. Soon enough I saw a number 19 bus approaching from Finsbury Park to the left. It trundled up through the traffic until it stopped at the bus stop, completely blocking my view. When it finally moved off, both Brandon and the girl were nowhere to be seen.

"That'll keep him occupied.." I said under my breath.

CHAPTER FOUR

Sharon Pennington

Brandon Stevens crossed the busy street at the first opportunity. He made a small jump to avoid a puddle then turned right and walked casually over to the bus shelter where the girl waited. After a quick glance to make sure she was still sitting inside, he leant against the outside of the perspex wall and pretended to browse his phone. He glanced at the girl occasionally to see she was chewing gum and appeared completely engrossed with her own phone. The empty sports bag she had been carrying was resting on her lap. Having seen her up close he was all the more convinced that she could be no more than fifteen years old. The story of the events from the previous evening and the video he had been shown weighed heavily on his mind as he stood there in the cold waiting for the bus. His concern for the unknown girl was made all the more poignant by the fact that at the age of 17, Brandon Stevens had lost his younger sister to cancer. She had been only 15 years old at the time and the girl he was now following bore a striking resemblance to her. Although Brandon Stevens kept up a facade of laddish bravado and cockney humour, he had been deeply affected by the death of his sister and still was to this day. It was a few minutes later when he looked up to see a number 19 bus approaching from Finsbury Park. It trundled through the traffic and came to a stop at the bus shelter. The young girl to his left stood up, slung the empty bag over her shoulder, and stepped onto the bus using the front door nearest the driver. She paid for her journey with coins from her handbag and made her way to a seat half way down the lower level of the double decker vehicle. Brandon Stevens waited for an elderly lady to board before doing the same and paying for his journey with a tap of his travel card. The doors closed with a loud hiss and the bus pulled off as he made his way back to find a seat. Once again, the girl was browsing her phone but as he approached she lifted her gaze from the screen and their eyes met for a split second. It was this brief moment that caused Brandon Stevens to feel a sudden and unexpected stab of pain in his heart.

It was not just the outward physical similarities. The young girl had striking green eyes very similar to those of his late sister.

Taking a seat some 3 metres back, he stared at the back of the girl's head and wrestled with the painful memories of his past. At the time he had been unable to protect his sister from the malevolent black crab that had slowly eaten away at her life. What Jason had suspected of going on in the flat above the kebab shop, and the video of the exchange with Ali the previous night troubled him deeply. Without knowing it, Brandon Stevens already felt a duty of care and protection over the young girl. He had no idea that this was something that would very soon place his life in grave danger. It was some 20 minutes later, as the bus was approaching the historic Islington Angel, that the girl stood up and got ready to disembark from the middle exit. The double door to the left opened with a hiss and she stepped out onto the street. Following from a distance, Brandon stepped off the bus and was greeted by a gust of icy wind blowing in from the South. As the girl walked off in the direction of the main Angel junction, she pulled the piece of paper she had been given by Zain from her handbag. After a brief pause, she turned left into Ritchie Street and made her way down the pavement on the left. From a distance of 30 metres, Brandon Stevens followed the girl turning left and passing a bakery and a busy deli. He noticed immediately that she walked with a youthful waddle and slightly duck feet; another trait that reminded him of his sister. The girl walked with purpose, clutching the piece of paper in her left hand and scanning the names of the shops around her as she went. It was as she reached the cul-de-sac at the end of the street that she crossed the tarmac and walked into the entrance of a large establishment by the name of Royal Garden Centre. There were a number of people congregated at the entrance and Brandon waited until the girl was out of sight before he entered. The large warehouse type building was well lit with wide aisles stacked with all manner of plants and gardening equipment. Piped music played softly through hidden speakers and it took some time for him to spot the girl who appeared to be wandering aimlessly down one of the aisles. Keeping his distance, Brandon picked up a packet of tomato seeds from a rack on his left and followed the girl. Eventually, seeming somewhat flummoxed, she walked up to an elderly man in overalls who was stacking a nearby shelf and showed him the paper.

The man smiled at her kindly and led her down the aisle to an open area at the rear of the building. He grabbed a trolley from a rack to the left and pushed it over to a large stack of heavy looking plastic bags near the back exit. After a brief conversation, the man lifted a single bag and placed it in the the trolley for the girl. He smiled again, pointed the girl in the direction of the exit, and made his way back to his work. Brandon waited until the girl had entered the building once again, then walked over to the stack which appeared to be 10 kg bags of lawn fertilizer of some sort. *Fertilizer?* He pulled his phone from his pocket, took a picture of the front of one of the bags, and followed the girl as she made her way back through the shop towards the tills. Pretending to be looking at a selection of sprinklers, Brandon watched as the girl paid for her purchase using the cash she had been given by Zain Usmani. She pulled the empty sports bag from her shoulder, placed the heavy bag of fertilizer inside, slung it over her shoulder, and headed for the exit. Placing the unwanted pack of tomato seeds on a shelf, Brandon waited until the girl had left the building before following once again. Her path led her back up Ritchie Street, across a busy zebra crossing, and straight to the bus stop opposite the one they had both arrived at not twenty minutes beforehand. Brandon watched as the girl walked into the bus shelter, placed the sports bag on the seat next to her, and sat down to wait. Leaning against a lamp post, he snapped a few pictures using his phone and waited. The bus arrived some 10 minutes later and the girl boarded and paid using coins once again. Not wanting to walk too far with the heavy bag, she took a seat near the front. Brandon followed and tapped his travel card to pay for the journey once again, but as he walked back through the bus the girl lifted her gaze and their eyes met once again.

Although it was only for a split second, a slight frown formed on her forehead when she saw him. He knew then that she had recognized him from earlier.

"Do I know you?" she said suddenly in a strong cockney accent.

Without thinking, Brandon stopped in his tracks and replied.

"I don't think so.." he said with a smile "But I saw you on the bus earlier."

"Oh.." she replied as the frown disappeared from her forehead "Sorry."

"No problem" said Brandon as he took a seat opposite the girl.

He knew then that there was no point in attempting to keep his distance and decided it may well be advantageous to continue talking to the girl.

"You from around here?" he asked casually.

"Yeah, Highbury.." she replied nonchalantly whilst looking at her phone "You?"

"Nah, I'm from South London, but I work in Highbury."

"Yeah?"

"Yeah, I work for the council.."

"Oh, okay.."

He reached forward with his right hand.

"Brandon Stevens" he said "Nice to meet you."

The girl lifted her eyes from her phone and there was a look of street wise suspicion on her face. This soon disappeared when she saw the open and genuine smile on Brandon's face.

"Sharon" she said shaking his hand "Sharon Pennington. Nice to meet you too.."

CHAPTER FIVE

Special Delivery

"You did what?" I said as Brandon climbed in the car and closed the door.

"I'm sorry, Jason" he replied panting slightly and looking nervous "Our eyes met as I got in the bus here and then again on the way back. She recognized me and asked if she knew me. I didn't know what to do, so I sat nearby and started a conversation.."

I took a deep breath as I thought through the implications of this unexpected development. *This could actually work in your favour, Green. You might be able to find out her age at least.*

"Well.." I said "There's nothing we can do about it now. So, where is she now?"

"She's there across the road.." came the reply "Waiting by the yellow door."

I turned to see the girl leaning against the door with the sports bag at her feet. There was a brief burst of sunshine which accentuated the grime on the greasy windows of the kebab shop.

"Okay.." I said "Tell me what happened. Where did she go?"

Brandon went on to narrate the journey to the Islington Angel and the garden centre. He told me of the purchase she had made and showed me the picture of the bag of fertilizer he had taken.

"What the *hell* is she doing buying that?" I said quietly "Send me that picture anyway please.."

Brandon went on to tell me her name and spoke about their conversation on the return journey to Highbury as I watched the girl waiting across the street. The sports bag lay at her feet as she browsed her phone. *What the hell is going here?* It was 5 minutes later when I saw the familiar Volvo approaching. As usual, it pulled into the alleyway to the left of the kebab shop and parked.

"Who's this now?" said Brandon.

His question was answered as the hunched figure of Zain Usmani climbed out of the vehicle holding his phone to his ear. At that very moment the girl's phone appeared to ring and she answered it immediately.

"He's calling her.." I said.

"Yeah, looks like it."

With the call over, Sharon Pennington reached down and lifted the heavy sports bag. At the same time Zain Usmani walked around and opened the back of the Volvo using the keys. He stood there in the grimy alleyway and waited for Sharon to arrive.

I lifted the binoculars to my eyes to get a closer look. The meeting was brief and we watched as the girl dumped the sports bag in the back of the Volvo. Zain leant forward and unzipped the bag to inspect its contents. Satisfied, he nodded curtly then stood to close the vehicle.

There followed a short conversation during which Zain handed the girl another banknote.

"He's paying her.." I said quietly "He sent her to go and get it."

"Why didn't he just go there himself?" said Brandon "Would have been much easier."

"Hmm.." I said "Very strange."

Sharon Pennington placed the banknote in her handbag as she walked out of the alley way. Turning left, she walked quickly past the kebab shop and the yellow door.

"She's on the move again" I said reaching for the ignition key "We'll follow in the car."

CHAPTER SIX

Zain Usmani

Zain Usmani parked the Volvo in the usual spot outside the family home. He walked around the back of the vehicle, opened it, and lifted the heavy sports bag. The weight of it caused the straps to dig into his thin shoulder as he walked towards the front door. It was with a sense of dread that he carefully unlocked the door and stepped into the hallway. Quietly, he placed the keys on the small table to his left. His prayers that his brief use of his father's car would go unnoticed went unanswered when he heard the booming voice coming from the lounge to the right.

"Bastard!" shouted his father, Akim "Where have you been in my car? Who gave you permission?"

Zain Usmani paused and bowed his head before looking into the brightly lit room from the base of the stairs. The towering figure of his father sat on the gaudy white faux leather sofa in front of a heavily ornate brass and glass coffee table. His bushy eyebrows were bunched in a frown and there were fires of anger in his dark eyes.

"I'm sorry father..." said Zain quietly "I needed to go to the shops for something. Please forgive me."

"Why don't you do something useful for once and clean that filthy hovel of yours?" growled his father "I can smell it from here!"

Zain Usmani was well used to the barrage of abuse from his father, but as usual, he bowed his head in shame.

"Yes father, I will do as you wish" he mumbled before making his way slowly up the stairs.

It was two flights of stairs up to his room on the top floor of the modest North London home. As Zain Usmani approached his heavily locked door he felt the usual sense of safety and calm he associated with his private space.

Lifting his grey tunic, he pulled a set of keys from his pocket and began opening the 3 heavy duty locks that secured his only sanctuary in the world. As he opened the door a waft of foul air engulfed him. It was the sweet sickly smell of body odour and dirty laundry, but it didn't bother him at all. In fact it was a great comfort, as for Zain Usmani this large single room was a haven of safety and peace. A private retreat far removed from the infidels of the world and the painful scorn of his family. It was also the epicentre of his private life and the place from which he had been planning his revenge on the cruel world that had branded him an outcast and a wretched untouchable. He grunted as he took the heavy bag from his shoulder and placed it on the cluttered table near his computer. Wasting no time, he turned and secured the locks on the inside of the door. It had been over 4 years since anyone had set foot in this private sanctuary of his and it was vital to Zain Usmani that he kept it that way. Finally, feeling 100% secure, he stepped up to the large desk and leant over to pull the string that activated the extractor fan he had installed in the window. It was with a growing sense of excitement that he closed the curtains, unzipped the sports bag and lifted the bag of fertilizer out of it. He felt a twinge of pain in his back as he placed it near the advanced chemistry set and lab equipment he had purchased online some months back. The bunsen burners, glassware, beakers, flasks, graduated cylinders, test tubes, and bottles stood neatly amongst the steel spatulas, stirring rods and clamps that made up his lab tools. The various chemicals and agents he had so carefully purchased were now all gathered in one place and it was finally time to get to work. Zain Usmani had built his very own bomb factory.

"Allahu Akbar.." he whispered to himself as he sat down on the work chair.

CHAPTER SEVEN

Appointment

Akim Usmani was fuming with anger as he glanced at his watch. The important meeting he had arranged for 1.30 pm at his house in Lower Holloway would have to be delayed for half an hour. He strode over to the sideboard, picked up his briefcase and car keys and stormed out of the front door of the house. The frigid December air engulfed him as he walked over to the Volvo station wagon and opened the door. His choice of vehicle had been deliberate and designed to give the impression that he was a humble family man with modest business interests. This was, of course, far from the truth as Akim Usmani was in fact an extremely wealthy man. As he climbed into the driver's seat of the car he was instantly surrounded by the lingering, sickly sweet stench of body odour. Suddenly he heard the familiar rushing sound of tinnitus in his ears. Similar to a howling gale, this would usually happen when he was angered or upset by something. Akim Usmani was aware that it was only he who could hear this strange sound, and for years it had troubled him. His anger issues ran deep and no matter how much he had fought to control them, they always seemed to return. He closed his eyes as he opened the driver's window to allow the smell to dissipate.

"Ya Ibn el Sharmouta..." he whispered to himself through gritted teeth. 'Son of a bitch.'

Akim Usmani sat for a moment and fought to control the hatred he felt towards his son, Zain. For 35 years, since the birth of his twins, he had attempted to hide the boy away behind closed doors in an effort to shield his family from the scorn of the community. Initially it had been easy, the troubled boy had been pampered by his mother and kept mostly out of sight. But for the past 10 years the boy had become increasingly religiously and culturally aware. Although the community smiled and nodded politely when he accompanied him to the Mosque, he could feel their sneering and in his mind this had brought a great amount of shame on his family. For years it had been easy enough to leave the boy to his own devices in his room on the top floor of the house.

A simple case of out of sight, out of mind. But recently this had changed and the resentment he felt was like a burning flame which he simply could not extinguish. Eventually the wave of anger passed and he opened his eyes and dialled a number on his phone.

"Marhaba, Kamil" he said quickly to the man who answered "I will be a little late, meet me at 2.00 pm..."

Akim Usmani started the engine of the Volvo and headed off towards the junction at Finsbury Park. Although the lunchtime traffic was busy, it took only 15 minutes to reach his double storey house in the leafy suburb of Lower Holloway. He locked the vehicle and after a quick look around, he let himself into the house after disabling the elaborate and expensive alarm system. The property had been purchased 10 years previously using a shelf company and its existence had remained a heavily guarded secret since then. Even his beloved son, Ali, had no idea that his father had purchased the property which he referred to as his private 'Safe House'. The construction work he had commissioned in the basement had taken 6 months to complete but since then only himself and a few very select number of 'customers' had ever set foot in the house. Akim Usmani opened the lounge door and peered in to take a look. The plain pine dining room table sat undisturbed in the centre of the room while the sheer curtains at the bay windows allowed pale daylight to filter in whilst blocking any scrutiny from the outside. The single LED light bulb that hung from the centre of the room was switched on as he had left it. Nodding in approval, he stepped back into the passageway and made his way back to the door beneath the staircase. Using a key from a smaller bunch in his pocket, he unlocked it, flicked a switch on the wall inside, and made his way down a set of steep wooden stairs to the basement below. The construction work he had commissioned in the basement involved the building of a thick partition wall that effectively split the subterranean area into two separate sections. In the centre of this wall was a thick steel door secured by two heavy sliding dead bolts. Using the same bunch of keys, he unlocked them both and pushed the heavy door inwards.

The single lightbulb that hung from the ceiling of this inner sanctum illuminated the sparse and simple furniture that consisted of a single chair and table with a commercial banknote counting machine on top of it. Set into the concrete of the far wall was a large safe with a combination mechanism to the front. He walked up to the safe and began twisting the dial to the left and right until he heard the click of the mechanism as it opened. The thick safe door opened on its hinges and it took a few seconds for his his eyes to adjust to the darkness of the interior. The top level of the safe had a steel drawer which contained a large amount of cash while the bottom area was open. Near the front of the space lay a black CZ 75 pistol while at the rear of the safe was a stack of 200 small brown rectangular briquettes. Measuring exactly 10cm by 1cm each, the highly compressed blocks of pure heroin from Pakistan had arrived 4 months ago. Their light brown colour and smooth consistency gave them an almost identical appearance to the ceramic tiles in which they had been so ingeniously hidden. Even the most advanced scanners could not detect any anomaly in their consistencies. The shipment had arrived in Dover in a container of decorative tiles from Pakistan and coffee from Kenya which had been added to the container at the port of Mombasa. The entire journey had taken 4 months from start to finish during which the pungent aroma of the coffee had slowly permeated the tiles, completely blocking out any airborne trace of the illicit cargo that had been so cleverly hidden within. For added security, the loaded tiles were carefully placed near the back of the container in amongst many thousands of other blanks. The only difference between the standard tiles and the loaded ones being a tiny notch that had been cut into the raw clay in the unglazed bottom surface of the tile prior to the firing process. A solid tap with a hammer was all that was needed to break the loaded tile and reveal the briquette of heroin hidden within. This ingenious process had been operating successfully for the past 12 years and had enabled Akim Usmani to build a substantial business empire. There had been, however, a mistake with the firing process on the last batch of tiles resulting in problems with the identification of the loaded tiles. The tiny notch that had been cut into the raw clay that marked them had been distorted by the heat of the firing ovens and had resulted in Akim Usmani having to destroy a third of the legitimate shipment in order to retrieve the heroin.

This had angered him greatly at the time and a stern warning had been sent to his partners in Lahore. To help mitigate the loss, a claim for goods damaged in transit had been filed with the insurers in London and he expected to be paid out in due course. Akim Usmani lifted the pistol and brought it out into the light. Its weight was reassuring and he turned in his hand to study it. Made in Czechoslovakia in the late 70s, he had bought it from a Albanian dealer some 10 years back. Having never had cause to use it, he closed his eyes and savoured the weight and feel of it in his hand. As he stood there he began to fantasize and his mind drifted to his son, Zain. *This would sort all your problems out once and for all. That abomination. That filthy masturbating bastard.* At that very moment the sound of rushing air in his ears returned. Suddenly his eyes opened wide in horror and he stared once again at the gun in his trembling hand. Despite the cold air in the basement, a trickle of sweat ran down his right temple and into his thick beard.

"Astaghfirullah..." he whispered through gritted teeth 'I seek forgiveness from Allah'.

Akim Usmani lifted his tunic and pushed the pistol under his belt. He knew full well he would not need the weapon but it was a precaution he took each time he met a customer. He reached into the safe, counted 11 of the briquettes and placed them on the table nearby. After locking the safe he lifted the small pile of briquettes, walked out of the room and up the stairs to the ground floor of the house. He closed the wooden door behind him and made his way into the sparsely furnished lounge. Before sitting down he opened his briefcase and placed a single briquette inside. This he would give to his beloved son, Ali. It offered him an opportunity to make some extra cash over and above his earnings from the kebab shop and also kept the young white whore happy. Glancing at his watch he sat down on one of the chairs that surrounded the simple pine table. The time was 2.06 pm and the customer he was due to meet was late. This would normally anger him greatly but given the fact that he too had been delayed, he decided to give Kamil a few more minutes. The familiar knock on the door came soon after and Akim Usmani walked into the hallway to let his guest in.

"As-Salam-u-Alaikum, Akim" said the short fat man who stood outside. 'Peace be unto you, Akim'.

"Wa-Alaikumussalam wa-Rahmatullah, Kamil" came the reply 'May the peace, blessings, and mercy of Allah be upon you, Kamil'.

The two men walked into the lounge and the legs of the pine chairs scraped on the bare floor boards as they sat. After a brief exchange of niceties, Akim Usmani pushed the pile of 10 briquettes across the table towards his customer. As he did so he saw the fat man's beady eyes light up. Although he had known Kamil for well over 5 years, he could sense the fear the man had for him, and he saw the tiny droplets of sweat forming on the man's forehead.

"Thank you Akim..." said the man as he reached into a bag hidden under his tunic "I have your envelope as usual."

The man placed a khaki envelope the size of a brick on the table then gathered up the briquettes.

"As usual" he said with with a sleazy grin "There is no need to count it..."

Akim Usmani grunted and watched as the man placed the briquettes into his bag. When he had finished he stood up, smoothed down his tunic, and smiled once again.

"Shukraan lak sayidi" said Kamil 'Thank you Sir.'

The two men said their goodbyes at the door and Akim Usmani descended once again to the secret room in the basement. Once there, he sat on the chair and ripped the tight plastic shrink wrapping from the brick of £50 bank notes. Although Kamil had said there was no need to count the money, Akim Usmani trusted nobody and he carefully fed wedges of the crisp notes into the money counter until the digital display confirmed that there was indeed £50000.00 in cash.

He gathered the money, shuffled it into a neat pile and stood to unlock the safe once again. Having placed the cash in the steel drawer to the top of the safe he took the pistol from his belt under his tunic. He held it in his hand briefly and stared at it wistfully before placing it once again in the bottom area of the safe. Five minutes later, Akim Usmani locked the front door of his Lower Holloway house, activated the alarm system, and drove off in in his Volvo station wagon.

CHAPTER EIGHT

Puzzles

Sharon Pennington walked quickly up the street past the shops. Across the road on her right were the winter faded fields of Highbury Park with its leafless trees and frost bitten lawns, while on the left stood a series of grand old Georgian mansions. Brandon and I followed in the hired car from fifty metres back, occasionally pulling into open parking spaces to allow the traffic to pass from behind. It was when she was nearing the boundary of the park that she turned left onto Pringle Street and began making her way downhill towards a series of ugly tower blocks below. She pulled her puffy pink jacket around her frame as she faced the wind and walked faster in an effort to beat the cold. It became clear soon after that we were leaving the pleasant suburb of Highbury and entering a significantly lower income area. The houses on either side of the street were unkempt and tatty and there was a distinct air of inner city urban decay to the place. We watched as she took a left turn at the base of the hill and made her way past a group of teenage boys who were loitering on the corner. Clutching tins of beer and wearing tracksuits with hoodies, they jeered her as she passed and I noticed Brandon tense up and wince as one of them flicked a cigarette butt in her direction. Ignoring them, she crossed the street and entered a grim looking council estate of towering 1970s high rise blocks. Once the pride of smart architects hoping to solve the housing crisis, these bleak edifices were now regarded as some of North London's ugliest buildings and were hotbeds of crime and drug abuse. Turning left at the base of the hill, I followed and made a right into a parking area near the entrance to the estate.

"She's going into the first block on the left..." said Brandon pointing towards the concrete space between the towering buildings.

"Hmm.." I replied as I watched her enter the massive building "The balconies are facing us. Lets try to see what floor she gets out on."

With the engine still running we gazed up at the grey facade of the building and waited for her to emerge onto one of the balconies. It was 3 minutes later when we saw the unmistakable flash of pink from the jacket appear on the 17th floor at the top of the block.

"There she is..." said Brandon pointing upwards.

Sharon Pennington made her way down the balcony until she reached the last flat on the left and disappeared inside.

"Well.." I said "Let's take a look around. Looks like a pretty rough area."

I locked the vehicle making sure to activate the alarm. Keeping an eye on the building, Brandon and I took a walk into the estate. The wet, grey concrete walls were covered in graffiti and the courtyard between the towering buildings was strewn with litter. To the right on the ground level was a laundrette, a small cafe, and a convenience shop.

"Keep an eye on the building, mate" I said "I'm just going to grab a packet of smokes."

The door to the shop squeaked loudly as I stepped inside and a sleepy looking woman with lank hair and hollow cheeks looked up from behind the counter. Immediately the small space was filled by the unsettling sound of a vicious dog barking from behind the counter.

"Toby!" screamed the woman in a cockney accent "Shut up, Toby!"

With the unseen dog placated, I stepped up to the counter and ordered the cigarettes.

Brandon stood shivering in the cold as I stepped out of the shop. What I had witnessed was bothering me and I felt I needed to keep further tabs on the girl.

I stood staring at the building as I ran through it all in my mind before finally making a decision.

"I think you should stay here for a while, Brandon" I said as I lit a cigarette "You can sit in the cafe here and keep an eye on things."

"Sure, Jason..." he replied "I can do that."

"If she comes out you can follow her, and if not I'll pick you up at around 5.00 pm."

"That's fine by me..." he replied.

We said our goodbyes and I made my way back to the vehicle past a group of rowdy children who were kicking a football around. As I drove up the hill towards Highbury there were a number of issues playing heavily on my mind. Firstly there was the girl, then the drugs, and finally the strange errand she had been sent on earlier that morning.

Fertilizer? What the hell would Zain want fertilizer for in North London? And even then, why would he send her to collect it? Although the kebab shop was open as I drove past, there was no sign of Ali's BMW so I decided to head to back to the family house in Finsbury Park. It was 20 minutes later when I arrived at my usual spot and parked the vehicle. The BMW was parked in its usual space but the Volvo station wagon was nowhere to be seen. It was then I noticed a curtain in an upstairs window opening. I lifted the binoculars to take a closer look and immediately saw the bearded face of Zain Usmani behind the glass. He appeared to be fiddling with an extractor fan mounted in the window frame and he closed the curtains soon after. *Well, Zain is back home.* I thought. *That means his father must have taken the Volvo.*

With nothing else to see, I picked up my phone and took a look at the picture Brandon had taken of the bags of fertilizer from the garden centre. The very fact that Zain had sent the girl to collect it seemed unusual and it was troubling me. I zoomed in on the picture to see it was a brand called 'Miracle Gro Multi Purpose Fertilizer' manufactured in Spain, it seemed much like any other product one might find in a garden centre.

Feeling puzzled, I looked up at the house and sighed deeply as I contemplated my next move. *You need to be 100% certain of what's actually going on in the flat above the kebab shop, Green. Then you need to ascertain the girl's age. If it is as you suspect, you'll need to report it to the police. Then you need to get on with the actual job you've been hired to do. This whole thing has distracted you. Concentrate.* I dropped my gaze to the phone once again and saw the picture Brandon had taken on the screen. With nothing else to do, I typed the words 'Miracle Gro Multi Purpose Fertilizer' into Google. A number of websites came up but I chose the manufacturer's own. It was as I scrolled down the page to the section that listed the chemical composition of the product that I saw the two words that caused me to sit up and sent an alarm bell ringing in my brain. Along with a number of other basic components, the product was primarily made up of a substance I was familiar with from my army days in Africa. When mixed with fuel oil it became highly unstable and when ignited with a small charge, it was capable of causing a massive explosion. That particular product made up 30% of the fertilizer and its name was listed clearly for all to see. Basically a salt of nitric acid, it was a product by the name of 'Ammonium Nitrate'. I let out a low whistle as I stared at the two words on the screen. *What is going here, Green?* At that moment the familiar Volvo station wagon passed me and I watched as it parked. The towering figure of Akim Usmani alighted from the vehicle carrying a briefcase. He walked swiftly to the front door of the house and disappeared inside.

CHAPTER NINE

Lab Rat

Zain Usmani was sweating with excitement as he pulled the string that activated the extractor fan in the window. He had no idea that he was being watched from a distance by an unknown stranger sitting in a car with a pair of binoculars. He pulled the curtains closed and flicked a switch on the wall that illuminated a bright neon light he had installed above his work space. Sitting down on his swivel chair he gazed at the many chemicals, pieces of hardware, and equipment he had so carefully gathered over the past few months.

"Allahu Akbar..." he whispered to himself.

He reached forward and clicked the mouse attached to his computer. Instantly the large screen came to life and Zain Usmani felt safe and at home once again. It had been 4 years since he had installed the powerful VPN software on the computer and ever since then he had been free to trawl the dark corners of the internet. It was there that he had been slowly and steadily radicalised. The virtual private network allowed him to communicate and share ideology openly with other esteemed scholars and warriors of Islam around the globe. It was deep within these hidden and encrypted websites and chatrooms that he had found himself and others like him, and it was there he had discovered his true calling. In his mind he had been dealt a cruel hand in the card game of life. His minor disabilities and weaknesses had caused even his beloved mother to distance herself from him. Although he saw her three times a day when she brought his food to the door, things were somehow different now. Despised and vilified by his own family and the world as a whole, it was here he had found solace, meaning, and purpose. The thousands of videos of religious sermons and teachings he had watched had informed and awoken him to his true principals and resolve. And it was there, in his private sanctuary, that he had set out on this journey that he had now almost completed. The hatred that had simmered and boiled within him would only be placated when he had fulfilled this mission, and that day would be soon.

But Zain Usmani was essentially a coward, and he had no intention of ending his own life with that final act. He had no interest in the 72 virgin maidens that awaited the courageous martyrs of Islam in paradise. In his mind they were reserved for the fornicators of *this* world. Filthy, slobbering, lustful monsters like his father and his much hated twin brother. The hours of instruction videos he had studied of the chemical and practical processes he was about to attempt were all available to him as references and finally it was time to build the device. A device that would detonate and rain down the very fires of hell on the infidels, and shatter the heart of the city. A trickle of sweat ran down his left temple as he gazed at the piles of supplies he had so carefully accumulated over the months. There was sodium bisulfate in the form of pool chemicals, sodium nitrate, potassium nitrate, calcium crystals, ammonia, methanol, distilled water and filters. All of these things had arrived from separate suppliers through mail order. Then there were the heavy bags of bolts and steel nails he had sent his brother's white whore to collect from the DIY store. The freon gas cannister he had ordered online, and a multitude of other components such as grinders, timers and fireworks with which to build fuses. But Zain Usmani's practical skills were somewhat hampered by his limited cognitive abilities and the processes he was about to embark on were complicated and potentially dangerous. The chemicals he would be mixing, amalgamating, heating, filtering and extracting were extremely unstable and volatile. But in his mind these were minor impediments and he would be guided and protected by God. He knew the process would be painstaking but he was prepared and would be careful and methodical. He had chosen the precise location of his target, London's Victoria Station, and over the course of three visits he had determined the perfect time at which to detonate the device. Zain Usmani took a deep breath and there was a sparkle in his otherwise dull brown eyes.

"Yes...." he said to himself quietly "It's time to get to work."

CHAPTER TEN

Ali Usmani

Ali Usmani stood up from the white faux leather sofa to greet his father as he placed his briefcase on the sideboard and walked into the lounge. The two men smiled at each other fondly and embraced in the centre of the room.

"Good afternoon, father.." said Ali quietly.

"My son..." came the reply "Come, let us sit and talk for a while."

The two men sat near each other and spoke in hushed tones until there was a quiet knock on the kitchen door.

"Come in.." said Akim in a booming voice.

The door opened and a short stocky woman shuffled in carrying an ornate silver tray with with two gilded glass cups of steaming Cardamom tea. Clad from head to toe in the traditional black hijab, she nodded respectfully at the two seated men before placing the tray on the glass centre table. Without a word she made her way back towards the kitchen door.

"Shukraan Amy" said Ali 'Thank you Mother'.

Akim Usmani waited until his wife had left the room before continuing the conversation. The two men drank tea and spoke about their various business ventures for the next 20 minutes until Ali glanced at his watch and stood up to excuse himself.

"My apologies Father.." he said "But I must get to work."

"Of course you must my son" said Akim as he stood up "I too must go to work at the warehouse this afternoon but your brother has delayed my day. By the way, I have something for you.."

The big man walked over to the sideboard and opened his briefcase. He took out the small compressed briquette of heroin and handed it to Ali.

"Kun Hadhiraan my son…" he said looking deep into his eyes 'Be careful my son'.

"Thank you, Father. Of course I will. Always…"

The two men embraced fondly once again and Akim Usmani followed his son to the front door and watched as he climbed into the BMW. He stood there until the car was out of sight then walked back into the lounge, picked up his briefcase, and he too left the house.

CHAPTER ELEVEN

South London

I watched as the Volvo station wagon turned around at the bottom of the street and passed my own vehicle at a sedate pace. Akim Usmani sat in the driver's seat staring ahead grim faced as he went. I started the engine of the hired car, did a quick U-turn and followed. The late afternoon traffic was easier than usual and it was fairly painless to keep up with him along the way. His route took him past the Islington Angel and then further South through the city to Farringdon station and across Blackfriars bridge on the River Thames. Although I had no idea where he was heading, I had suspected he was on his way to his South London warehouse. It was 4.00 pm and a light patter of rain started falling from the gun metal sky above as we arrived at the entrance to the sprawling Stone Industrial Estate. Lined with trees in an effort to beautify an otherwise drab business park, the estate was comprised of a series of avenues dotted with medium sized factory units. There were builders merchants, plumbing supply companies, signwriters, and a hundred other small businesses within the green palisade fences of the industrial park. Akim Usmani parked his Volvo outside a blue corrugated steel building at the far end of the estate. I parked my own vehicle some 50 metres away near a forklift hire company and turned off the engine as I watched. The big man got out of his vehicle carrying his briefcase and quickly made his way to the front door of the building through the rain. Above the entrance to the building was a discreet sign that read 'Akus Trading' with a phone number and website address underneath. It was clear to me that this was an abbreviation of his own name. I opened the file I had been given by the insurance company to see that this was indeed the same factory the assessor had visited when the claim had first been filed. The brief description I had been given stated that the company was involved in the importation of decorative ceramic tiles from Pakistan and coffee from Kenya. With nothing else to do at the time I typed the web address of the firm into my phone. The company website was fairly plain and only consisted of a few pages showing off their products, but it was as I was browsing their selection of decorative ceramic tiles that I had an idea. I dialled the phone number on the sign in front of me and waited for an answer.

"Akus Trading, good afternoon" came the cheerful reply from what sounded like a young Asian lady.

"Oh, hello.." I said "Could I speak to someone in sales please?"

"I can help you sir.."

"Okay, great..." I said "I'm actually on your website right now, and I'm interested in your tiles. I'm opening a restaurant in the city and I'm looking for around 300 square metres of them for the flooring."

"Yes sir" she replied "We can certainly help you there. Would you be able to come down to our warehouse in South London some time? We have a small showroom and I can show you our selection."

"Sure I can. I'll come tomorrow around midday if that's alright, is it the address on the website?"

"That's correct sir, my name is Samaira and I'll be glad to show you our range."

"Super.." I said "My name is Jason Green. I'll give you a call when I'm on my way down there."

I hung up after saying goodbye to the lady and looked around for a sheltered spot in which to have a cigarette. There was nowhere apart from the overhang at the entrance to the forklift hire company to my left. It was only then that I noticed the two men sitting in the white transit van on the opposite side of the road to my right. Although the vehicle had been there since I had arrived, I had simply assumed it had been parked and left there. Both seemingly in their forties, the two men were dressed in blue overalls and sat staring at me with frowns on their foreheads. It was almost as if I was trespassing and had no right to be there.

Knowing full well I had every right to be there, I smiled at the men and raised my right hand to greet them. This cheerful gesture only served to upset them further and their frowns quickly turned into angry scowls. Feeling somewhat puzzled by this unusual confrontation, I lifted both hands in a questioning gesture and silently mouthed the words 'What's the problem?' The man in the driver's seat turned and spoke to his companion briefly before opening the door of the vehicle and walking over towards me. *What now?* A blast of freezing wind blew into my vehicle as I opened the window to speak to the approaching man. Short and stocky with a round face and cropped grey hair, the man walked swiftly across the road with the same angry look on his face.

"May I ask what you're doing here Sir?" he said in an unexpectedly well spoken accent.

"Minding my own business.." I said incredulously "Who the hell are you?"

The man frowned impatiently and glanced towards the business premises of Akim Usmani. He reached into the top pocket of his overalls and pulled out a worn brown leather wallet which he opened and held up for me to look at. The shiny crown capped badge of the Metropolitan Police was mounted into the left hand side of the wallet.

"Thames Valley Police, sir" he said quietly "May I ask what you're doing here?"

"Oh, I'm sorry officer.." I said "I just stopped to make a call."

"Right sir..." said the man "Now, if you wouldn't mind moving along.."

"Sure.." I replied as I started the engine "Sorry."

The man thanked me politely and walked back to the van as I drove off. I took another look at the van in my rear view mirror as I drove.

Unmarked and painted plain white, there was nothing about it that looked out of place in an industrial park. *What the hell are they doing here?* I thought. I followed the exit signs for the estate until I made it out of the main gate and took a right turn heading back to North London. There was no doubt in my mind that the two policemen were on an undercover assignment and were there watching the very same building I had been. *A plain white van parked near where I parked. Both vehicles with an open view of Akus Trading. There's a lot more going here than you think, Green. A lot more...*

CHAPTER TWELVE

Ali Usmani

Ali Usmani was feeling tense and unsettled as he parked his BMW in the alley and took the short walk to the take away.

"Afternoon boss!" said the young manager of Supreme Kebabs as he walked in.

"Alright lads..." he replied quietly as he made his way around the front counter and into the rear of the building where his office was located.

Feeling somewhat stressed, he pulled a set of keys from his shell suit, opened the door, and let himself into the office, locking the door behind him. The room was cheaply decorated with faux gold framed pictures of sports cars and speedboats. Taking his seat behind the expansive desk, he pulled the small briquette of heroin from his pocket and placed it in front of him. He opened the top left drawer of the desk and pulled out a mirror, a digital scale, and other bits of drug paraphernalia. Using a Stanley knife, he cut a neat 1 centimetre cube from the corner of the briquette, weighed it on the scale, and placed it in a small resealable plastic bag. *That'll keep the young whore happy.* After pocketing the bag he stood up and walked over to the small wall safe to the left hand side of the room. He punched a code into the digital panel to the front of the safe and opened the small door. The interior of the small safe was made up of three shelves. The top one was filled with bundles of cash while the middle one had only a small but tightly packed plastic bag of white powder. Ali Usmani's cocaine habit was an extremely well guarded secret, especially from his father, and he knew full well the potential for furious disapproval and punishment should it ever be discovered. His father had taught him that all drugs were the filthy vices of the infidels and unbelievers of the world and for them, they should always remain simply a means to an end. A business product. He placed the briquette of heroin on the lower shelf of the safe and removed the small bag of cocaine.

Leaving the safe door open, he walked back to his desk, sat down, and tipped a small pile of the white powder onto the mirror. With a deft hand and a credit card, he quickly cut the pile into into two thick symmetrical lines. Using a crisp £20 note which he rolled up, he leant forward and snorted both lines, one up each nostril.

Ali Usmani sat back in the chair with his eyes closed and thumbed at his nose in order to dislodge any scraps of the powder that may have become trapped in his nostril hairs. As he did so, the thick gold chain on his wrist clicked and rattled. Slowly but surely the familiar feelings of intense pleasure and euphoria returned and Ali Usmani felt on top of the world once again. He opened his eyes to look around the room and blinked as the drug took effect and his pupils dilated. Using a remote control on the desk he turned on a stereo and the sound of loud electronic dance music suddenly filled the room. He sprung to his feet and walked over to a wall mirror mounted on the back of the door. With his head nodding to the beat of the music he ran his hands through his hair and studied his face in the reflection. He turned his head in order to admire the side profile of his neatly trimmed beard and watched his jaw muscles bulge as he chewed the gum in his mouth. Satisfied his appearance was in order he brought up his right hand, smiled brightly, and pointed at himself in the mirror.

"You're the king of North London.." he said to himself in his cockney accent "Yep. Cream of the crop, mate."

Ali Usmani spun around on his expensive trainers and walked back to his desk. He replaced the mirror and the other paraphernalia in the drawer and picked up the bag of white powder. It was as he was placing it back in the safe that he remembered the debt owed to him by his associate, Rashid Abdelrahman. Based in the suburb of Muswell Hill, Rashid was a low level drug dealer who had been buying small amounts of heroin from him for the past 2 years. But it had been in the past 4 months that Rashid had become erratic with payments and had been asking for credit. Ali had initially agreed to extend credit but recently he had come to believe that Rashid may have developed a habit of his own. Chewing the gum furiously, Ali gazed at the pile of cash on the upper level of the safe. Lying next to it was a single piece of paper with a cash amount written on it. He took the paper from the safe and stared at what he had written.

"Rashid , £3000.00..." he said to himself as he read the note "That's a lot of cash and it's been too long now. He's gotta pay up..."

Ali Usmani locked the safe and returned to the comfortable seat behind his desk. He pushed his chair back, put his feet up on the desk, and dialled the number for Rashid. The young man answered immediately and Ali turned the volume of the music down on the remote control.

"Hello mate..." he said in a kindly voice "Just checking on that three grand you owe me. Been a while now."

There followed an exhaustive ten minute back and forth conversation where a number of excuses and sincere apologies were made from Rashid. Finally it was agreed that Rashid would visit the flat above the kebab shop the following morning at 9.30 am to discuss a payment plan for the monies owing. Satisfied the matter would be amicably resolved, and still buzzing intensely from the two massive lines of cocaine, Ali Usmani sat back and smiled. He turned the volume up on the stereo once again and sat with his eyes closed as he listened to the repetitive beat. *Ahh yes.* He thought. *Life is good.* A minute later he sat forward, opened his laptop computer, and logged onto his favourite porn site.

CHAPTER THIRTEEN

Spy Cam

The rush hour traffic on the drive back to North London was heavy and it was completely dark by the time I reached the Islington Angel. It was at the traffic lights at the main junction when I was finally able to call Brandon.

"Where are you, mate?" I asked.

"Hey, Jason" he replied "I'm still at the cafe, I wasn't sure what to do and I didn't hear from you.."

I glanced at my watch to see it was 5.45 pm and I had told him I would collect him at 5.00.

"Sorry Brandon, I got caught up in South London and the traffic is crazy. Has the girl moved yet?"

"No problem, and no, not yet. I've been here the whole time drinking tea and watching the building. She hasn't come out yet.."

"Well.." I said "It's late, I think you can call it a day. I can pick you up if you like?"

"No need. It's a short walk up the hill and I'll get a bus from there."

"Okay, well in that case we can meet as usual at my place tomorrow at 8.00 am.."

"Sure.." he replied "I'll see you then."

It was 6.00 pm by the time I parked the hire car and headed up to the 5th floor of my apartment block. As I stood in the lift, a number of bewildering and unanswered questions were swimming around in my mind. First was the girl, Sharon Pennington, her true age, and what exactly was going on in the flat above the kebab shop. Secondly was the fact that I had witnessed Ali Usmani giving her drugs of some kind. Then there was the unusual mission she had been sent on by Zain Usmani to the garden centre and the fact that she had collected a product primarily made up of Ammonium Nitrate.

Lastly was the fact that I had accidentally run into two undercover policemen at the main business premises of Akim Usmani. I had no doubt they had placed Akus Trading under surveillance and my presence there had rattled them. But then there were the ever present doubts. *So many questions, Green. You think there is a lot more going on here than meets the eye, but then again, it may well be that all of this is entirely innocent? Maybe young Sharon Pennington is above the age of consent and there is no knocking shop above the takeaway. What if it wasn't actually drugs she was handed by Ali? It could be that the strange looking son, Zain, is a keen gardener after all. Maybe those cops were just taking a break and having a late lunch? Perhaps it's just you and you're simply being paranoid?* The doors of the lift opened and I took the short walk down the balcony to the door of my 5th floor flat as I wrestled with these thoughts. It was a relief to step into the warmth after the arctic chill outside but I knew there was no time to waste. *You need answers, Green. Trust your gut instincts here.*

There's only one way to get those answers. Start at the beginning. Without removing my jacket I walked into my bedroom and retrieved and pocketed the small pouch of surveillance equipment I needed from the cupboard. I stood in the lounge and summoned an Uber from my phone. As luck would have it there was one nearby and once again I made my way out into the frozen night. The car was waiting as I exited the building and it only took 20 minutes to get to the pub. The portly barman recognized me from the previous night and began pulling my pint as I walked up to him. I paid him for the drink, took the same seat near the windows, and sat down to watch the proceedings. The BMW of Ali Usmani was parked in its usual spot in the alley way to the left of the building but as usual, he was nowhere to be seen. The take away itself was busy with a steady stream of customers coming and going but there was no light in the windows of the flat above. The niggling doubts I had been feeling began creeping back as I sat sipping the beer and fighting the urge to smoke a cigarette. *Maybe you're wrong, Green. Maybe this whole conspiracy thing is just in your mind. You'll have wasted a whole lot of time and you will certainly feel like a fool if it is.* But my fears were allayed when 20 minutes later, Sharon Pennington returned. As she had done the night before, she walked on the opposite side of the street and waited near the yellow door.

Like before, she stood out from the rest of the sensibly dressed pedestrians with her bright pink jacket and tight white leggings. *Here we go, Green.* Ali Usmani appeared a minute later from behind the counter of Supreme Kebabs. Wearing another flashy shell suit, he walked out, opened the door for the girl, and returned to the shop. Seconds later the lights in the upstairs flat were turned on and their dull glow through the tatty red curtains gave the building a distinct look of decay and seediness. Leaving my beer on the table, I walked out into the frozen night and stood in the darkness under the canopy for a cigarette. It was then that the first man arrived. I recognized him immediately from the previous night and as before, he made his way upstairs alone. I took a photograph of him when he emerged and left some 20 minutes later. Over the next few hours there followed an almost carbon copy of the events of the previous evening with all four men, including Akim Usmani, visiting the flat above the takeaway. I managed to take photographs of them all as they came and left until, at around 10.00 pm, the lights went out in the upstairs apartment, and Sharon Pennington emerged from the yellow door. By then the staff in the takeaway were busy closing shop and tidying up after the day's trade. Ali Usmani appeared soon after and once again he met her briefly on the pavement and surreptitiously handed her a tiny bag. She quickly put it in her handbag and walked off in the direction she had come from. The barman called time at around 10.30 pm and it was then that the lights went out in the takeaway across the street. Ali Usmani locked the premises after the staff had left and I watched him reverse out of the alley way as he headed home. I made my way outside and stood in the darkness nearby to wait for an opportune moment to make my move. With the street almost empty and the punters having left the pub, I crossed over and slipped into the alley way. Once again there was the overpowering stench of rotting food waste from the rubbish bins and I stood at the gate in the wooden fence to allow my eyes to adjust to the darkness. When they finally did I saw the small padlock that secured it. Seeing no point in attempting to pick it, I simply pushed one of the smaller plastic rubbish bins up to the fence and climbed over. The back yard of the kebab shop was paved with concrete and strewn with plastic buckets of used cooking oil and other food packaging waste. To the centre of the back wall the heavy old drain pipe rose up to the second floor of the building.

Rubbing my hands together vigorously to beat the cold, I walked up to it and pulled at it in order to check it was firmly attached to the brickwork. Satisfied it was, I began climbing it using the ridges in the metal as grips and the old wooden wall brackets as footholds. The paint on the surface of the old metal pipe was blistered, and by the time I had reached the windows at the second floor my hands were chaffed and aching. Still clinging to the pipe with the wind howling in my ears, I placed my right foot on the window ledge of what I assumed to be the bathroom and began working on the old sash window. Although I tried to lift it from both sides, the old window clearly hadn't been opened in years and appeared to be firmly stuck in the closed position. I reached into my jacket pocket with my right hand and retrieved the stubby screwdriver I had brought. I jammed it into the base of the old wooden frame and put my weight behind it as I tried to lever the window upwards. At that moment I heard the old drain pipe creak under my weight and a sprinkling of dust fell on my face from the wall bracket above. *This old drain is gonna give way, Green. Best you get that window open now or there could be a nasty accident.* Panting heavily from the exertion, I turned my head and looked at the 5 metre drop below. A fall from that height would not be fatal but would surely result in a few broken bones on the concrete below. Immediately, my vision began to swim and spin and my legs tingled as the vertigo kicked in. Unable to move, I gritted my teeth and screwed my eyes shut until it passed. With a final effort, I shifted more of my body weight onto the handle of the screw driver and finally heard the faint cracking sound of the window lifting in its frame. It took a full minute of grunting and lifting but finally I had pushed it up by 3 feet and I carefully climbed from the drainpipe onto the ledge and inside. The interior of the room was pitch black and I almost fell over the old sink that was directly beneath the window. Feeling my way, I eventually made it onto what felt like a tiled floor and sat down panting heavily with my eyes closed. The first thing that struck me was the smell. It was a mixture of urine, mould, and damp. I reached into my pocket and retrieved a penlight torch which when switched on revealed I was sitting on the floor in a bathroom. The fittings were ancient and yellowed and the tiled floor I sat on was chipped and cracked.

It looked to me that the room had last been renovated in the 1940s. As I stood up I became more and more aware of the stench of the place. The old cast iron bath was stained yellow and brown and one of the taps dripped constantly. The front left corner of the old china sink was broken rendering it useless and the toilet was missing its seat. A rusted pipe ran up the wall to an old fashioned cistern and chain pull mechanism mounted above. Floating in the water of the blackened toilet bowl was a used condom. Whoever had dumped it there had been reluctant to pull the chain and I can't say I blame him given how filthy the room was. With my stomach beginning to turn, I pushed the door open and stepped into the small corridor beyond. Once again, the walls were yellowed with peeling paint and the fitted carpets below were speckled with decades of dust and filth. I turned my head and looked into the kitchenette which was no better. The sink was filled with empty beer cans and apart from an old kettle and a few mugs, there was very little in there and most of the cupboard doors were either missing or loose. I walked quietly down the corridor and pushed the far door open. The lounge area was furnished with a threadbare suite and an old wooden coffee table to the centre. The walls were covered in tatty old 1970s wallpaper that was a dull orange colour with psychedelic geometric designs. The room smelt damp and musty and there were a number of ashtrays scattered around that were filled with cigarette butts. The curtains at the window that faced the street were a dusty red colour and the only modern appliance in the room was a large stereo that sat on a sideboard to the left of the room. I walked back down the corridor and opened the bedroom door. Once again, a wall of foul smelling air hit me but this time it was a combination of body odour and the sickly sweet smell of moisturising cream and lubricants. The walls were a light blue colour but the paint was grubby and peeling in spots. To the left of the room was an unmade double bed. Its centre springs having long since collapsed, there was a stained duvet bunched up to the centre of it along with an equally soiled sheet and a few pillows. Once again my stomach churned as I stepped inside the room. A single bare lightbulb hung from a wire in the centre of the ceiling. I walked up to the window and carefully pulled the red curtain to one side. The view across the street to the pub was clear and I saw the table I had been sitting at not half an hour before. Next to the bed was single drawer with an ashtray on top of it.

I walked over, opened the top drawer, and shone the beam of the torch inside. Lying there in plain view was a single teaspoon with a blackened bowl, a section of surgical tubing, and a number of syringes and needles. There was no longer any doubt whatsoever in my mind. *These are the tools of a junkie, Green. And this can only be for heroin.* It was standing in such close proximity to the bed that made me realise the source of the stench. It was the filthy mattress and bedding that caused me to gag and cough as I closed the drawer and stepped back to get away from it. *Jesus Christ, Green. This is fucking awful.* Feeling a desperate urge to get out of the hovel I had found myself in, I blinked and shone the torch around the room. Behind me was an old wardrobe with a cracked mirror to the front. I turned and looked at it to see the scrolled wooden decoration to the top of it would provide a perfect spot for the miniature camera. I ran my finger across the top of the cupboard and it came as no surprise to see it come away covered in dust. *Perfect.* I pulled the tiny Japanese device from my pocket and removed a section of double sided tape from beneath it. The slimline Lithium battery would remain unseen behind the wood at the front of the cupboard while the tiny motion activated camera would sit on top and would automatically record and stream any sound or movement in the room for as long as the battery life held out. Slowly and methodically, I activated and placed the tiny camera in position. Satisfied it would remain unseen, I logged into the camera's mobile app on my phone and waited until I saw myself standing there on the screen.

"Testing, 1, 2, 3.." I said quietly.

Although slightly tinny on the small speaker on my phone, I heard my voice clearly. *Good, now for the lounge.* I repeated the process in the lounge using the pelmet above the curtains as the hiding place for the second camera. Once I was certain both cameras were concealed well and functioning correctly, I took a final look around to see if there was anything I might have missed. Finally I decided I had seen enough. I made my way back to the bathroom and carefully climbed out of the window onto the ledge. By then a light pattering of freezing rain was falling which further added to my anxiety about slipping and falling, and I purposely kept my eyes to the wall in front of me rather than looking down.

Gripping the drain pipe with my left hand, I forced the sash window closed once again using my right foot. Thankfully the drain pipe held fast and I made my way down safely to the concrete below. Using a pile of empty cooking oil drums I scaled the wooden fence and jumped back down onto the wet cobbles below. I had summoned an Uber cab by the time I made it back to the street and stood shivering and smoking a cigarette under the shop front of Supreme Kekabs as I waited. The drive home took only 10 minutes at that late hour and it was with great relief that I finally stepped into the warmth of my 5th floor apartment. The stench of the flat above the takeaway seemed to linger in my nostrils and it was as if the very fact that I had been in there had somehow tainted me. I immediately headed for a long hot shower where I scrubbed my body forcefully in an effort to wash away the memory of it. Finally I lay down on my bed with a myriad of thoughts swimming through my mind. Even given what I had seen inside the flat, I consoled myself with the knowledge that I had taken the first step towards establishing and proving it. *This is a rotten bunch of people, Green. Take one step at a time and you'll prove it*. Although I was tired, it took some time for sleep to come to me that night and when it did, it was fitful and disturbed by the strange and unusual events of previous two days.

CHAPTER FOURTEEN

Arrears

Ali Usmani was feeling slightly nauseous and a bit shaky as he walked into the lounge of the family home. The time was 8.30 am and his father was seated in his usual place on the sofa.

"Good morning my son" said Akim in his deep, booming voice "Come and share some food with me."

"Sorry Father.." said Ali "I'm not hungry this morning, but I will sit and have some tea with you."

Akim Usmani frowned and studied his son as he took a seat on the sofa nearby. He seemed somewhat twitchy and irritated, and his usual healthy glow was faded and ashen.

"What is it that is bothering you, my son? You seem troubled" he said as he poured a cup of cardamom tea.

In reality, Ali Usmani was suffering from a classic cocaine come down. He had tossed and turned all night and hardly slept at all. At that moment he wished he had brought a small amount of his secret stash home. It would have given him the boost he needed to get the day started and appear normal. Now he found himself confronted by his father whose piercing eyes studied him intently, and they were eyes that saw through most things. Ali Usmani needed an excuse and he needed one fast. He shifted uncomfortably in his seat as he thought.

"It's just a minor problem with business, Father" he replied "Nothing I can't handle."

"Perhaps it is a problem with money?"

"Well, yes it is. I have a customer, Rashid Abdulrahman from Muswell Hill."

"And what is the problem with this Rashid from Muswell Hill, my son?"

"Well, it's money, Father. The man owes me £3000.00."

"And for how long long has this Rashid owed you this money?"

"It's a few months now, Father. He keeps making excuses and promises, but the money is still owed."

"And what are you doing to rectify this situation?"

"Well, he has agreed to come to meet me this morning at the flat above the shop. We will discuss a payment plan. I'm sure it will be fine..."

Akim Usmani glared at his son as he passed him the steaming cup tea. He noticed his hand shook slightly as he took it. The sight of his beloved son in such a troubled and anxious state pained him deeply, and he decided at that moment that he would step in to assist.

"What time is this Rashid from Muswell Hill meeting you my son?" he said.

Ali Usmani blinked at the shock of the hot liquid on his tongue. He reached forward and placed the steaming mug on the glass table. His shaking hand caused the mug to rattle on the glass table.

"He will be there at 9.30 this morning, Father."

Akim Usmani sat back and stared at his son thoughtfully.

"Very well..." he said "I too will be there waiting for this Rashid. And I will teach you how we deal with bad debtors."

A cold pang of fear and alarm spread through Ali Usmani's body as he sat back in his seat. He knew full well the potential for furious anger his father was capable of, but he also knew not to argue with him at this point. He knew there was absolutely nothing he could do or say at that point and he dropped his gaze sullenly to the floor.

"Very well, father..." he said quietly.

CHAPTER FIFTEEN

Appointment

It was 8.30 am when Brandon Stevens and I walked out of my apartment and took the lift down to the ground floor. The morning was bright, clear, and bitingly cold. He had arrived on time as promised and after a cup of coffee, had happily agreed to my plan of having him watch the premises of Supreme Kebabs for the morning. I had explained that I had made an appointment at Akus Trading in South London later that morning but told him nothing about my movements from the previous night, choosing to keep that to myself for the time being. Although I was pretty certain what was going on in the flat above the takeaway, I had decided that definitive proof was better than mere speculation. And that proof would surely come later that night. My main concern was the true age of Sharon Pennington, but this was something I would attempt to find out as well. It was exactly 9.00 am when I pulled over and parked near the bus stop at the Queen's Head pub.

"I've been thinking about the girl, Brandon" I said "I don't think it's such a bad thing that you ran into her yesterday, it might actually work in our favour. You mentioned she was quite friendly?"

"Yeah, she was..."

"Well listen.." I replied "If you see her at any stage today, why not try to engage her in another casual conversation? Try to find out her age."

"Ah, well..." he replied with a guilty look "I actually know she's only 15 years old, Jason."

"How do you know that?" I asked.

"Well, I looked her up on Facebook last night..."

"I see, and you're sure it's her?"

"I'm one hundred percent sure, Jason. Sorry, I should have mentioned it.."

"No, that's fine" I said thoughtfully. "Well done, that's good work. I still think it might be a good idea to try strike up a conversation if you do see her. It can't do any harm and we might be able to glean some more information about the Usmani family."

This idea seemed to appeal to young Brandon and his face lit up at the prospect.

"Keep it casual, of course" I said "Just a friendly chat..."

"Yeah, no problem Jason" he replied enthusiastically "Don't worry, I'll do my best.."

With everything finalized, we said our goodbyes and I drove off looking for a gap in the traffic in which to do a U-turn. It was 9.20 am when I arrived back at my apartment and flicked the switch on the kettle to make some coffee. I walked into the lounge and opened my laptop while I waited for it to boil. The pale winter sun shone through the bay windows bathing the space in a rare warm glow. My appointment at Akim Usmani's factory in South London was for midday so I had some time to kill. *Well, you're finally getting somewhere Green. Moving forward instead of spending all day in the car. Perhaps this job will be wrapped up sooner than you think.* It was as I walked back into the lounge with the coffee that I saw the tiny flashing icon for the hidden cameras flashing on the bottom right of the laptop screen. I knew the only way they could have been activated was by movement or activity in the flat. *Oh yes, what's going now?* I quickly sat down and clicked on the icon to open up the view. The screen expanded to show the camera I had placed in the lounge was indeed streaming live video. Seated on the sofas in the lounge of the flat were two men I instantly recognized as Akim and Ali Usmani. Although I could clearly see their lips moving, I could not hear what they were saying. Using the mouse pad, I adjusted the volume on the computer until I could hear them talking clearly.

"Well, good morning gentlemen.." I said to myself after a sip of coffee "What's going on today?"

CHAPTER SIXTEEN

Rashid Abdulrahman

Ali Usmani was in a cold sweat and he shifted nervously in his seat as he waited for the door bell to ring. He glanced at his watch every 30 seconds knowing full well his father was a stickler for time keeping and would likely become angry should Rashid be late for their appointment. His father sat opposite him, calmly drumming his fingers on the threadbare arm of the sofa. Although Ali could not be certain, he was convinced his father was studying him, and had been since they had left the family house and arrived at the flat above the takeaway. *Calm down.* He told himself. *You're being paranoid. Everything will be fine.* It was at 9.30 am on the dot when a loud buzzer sounded in the corridor. The sound of it caused Ali to jump. Thankfully, Rashid Abdelrahman had made it on time.

"That's him, Father" said Ali with relief as he stood up.

Akim Usmani nodded calmly and said nothing as his son rushed downstairs to open the yellow door. A rush of freezing air blew into the darkened stairwell as he opened the door. Twenty eight year old Rashid Abdulrahman stood there alone with a lazy smile on his face. His short black hair was gelled and combed down and he wore what looked like an expensive Ralph Lauren jacket. The first thing Ali noticed was the gold stud earring Rashid wore in the lobe of his left ear. The sight of it caused him a twinge of anxiety as he knew full well his father would disapprove of it. The second thing he saw were the constricted pupils in Rashid's bloodshot eyes. A clear sign of heroin abuse.

"Alright mate?" said Rashid with a slight slur.

Ali Usmani knew then that his visitor was completely wired, and this caused further alarm bells to ring in his head.

"Listen, Rashid!" he hissed "My father is up there. You be be cool, okay?"

"Oh, yeah.." came the slurred reply "No worries mate."

The two men made their way up the stairs and into the lounge of the small flat.

"Father.." said Ali nervously "This is Rashid."

Akim Usmani stood up calmly and walked towards Rashid who had entered the room. His tall frame towered above the young man who offered a limp handshake and a lethargic greeting.

"Nice to meet you sir" he mumbled quietly.

Akim Usmani motioned towards the sofa on the opposite side of the small room.

"Please.." he said in his deep silky voice "Take a seat, Rashid."

The young man sat down with a dreamy smile and nodded slowly at his hosts.

Akim Usmani sat down and pulled gently at his beard as he studied the young man who sat opposite him. The silence in the room was broken only by the sound of traffic on the street below the single window. Ali sat biting his nails as he waited for someone to break the silence of the impasse.

"Thank you for coming to see us today, Rashid.." said Akim calmly.

"Yeah, no worries.." came the vague reply.

"I understand there is an amount of money owing to my son, Ali?"

"Yeah, yeah.." said Rashid dreamily "I'm really sorry about the delay. That's why I came to talk to you about it"

"I see. And have you brought any of the amount owing here today?"

"Yeah!" said Rashid "I brought £300."

Akim Usmani nodded at Ali who stood up and walked over to the clearly intoxicated young man. Rashid stretched his legs out where he sat and groped in his jeans pocket as he tried to retrieve his wallet. Eventually he pulled it out and began slowly counting bank notes. All the while Akim watched the proceedings silently as his anger grew. Soon enough the familiar rushing sound of wind in his ears returned as he studied the hapless young man. The earring the man wore, the gold ring on the pinkie finger of his right hand, his glazed bloodshot eyes and his general sloppy and casual attitude. All of these things maddened him and as much as he fought it, the howling winds of rage he heard would not cease. It was only when the full £300 had been counted out and handed to Ali, that Akim lifted his gaze and spoke to his son.

"My son" he said "Would you please turn that stereo on and play some music?"

Ali stared back at his father with a puzzled look on his face.

"Music.." he said quietly "Would you please play some music now?"

Feeling somewhat confused, Ali walked over the stereo in the corner of the room. Using the remote control he turned it on and immediately the room was filled with the pounding, repetitive sound of British grime rap music. Rashid Abdulrahman smiled and looked up at the figure of Ali standing in the corner. The corners of his mouth were white and gummed with dried saliva.

Akim Usmani rose to his feet and walked to the centre of the room.

"Thank you for coming, Rashid" he said over the music.

He held out his right hand in an offer of a handshake. The bewildered young man smiled, stood up and stepped forward with own his hand outstretched. It was only when their two hands met that Akim Usmani struck. With a vice like grip, he yanked the smaller man towards him while at the same time bringing his open left hand around towards Rashid's head with lightning fast speed. The sound of the blow was like a gun shot and immediately the stunned body of Rashid Abdulrahman collapsed in a heap on the filthy carpet below.

Wasting no time, Akim Usmani knelt down placing the full weight of one knee on the back of the neck of the semi conscious man. The other knee went down in the middle of his back, effectively pinning him to the ground. Within a second, Akim Usmani lifted his tunic and pulled a pair of long nosed pliers from his pocket. At that moment the man on the floor let out a muffled moan as he regained consciousness. Akim Usmani lifted the man's left arm up and held it there while he gripped his thumb. By then the forlorn moaning was becoming louder and decidedly panicked. Akim turned to his stunned and speechless son who still stood near the stereo in the corner of the room.

"Turn up the volume, Ali!" he said firmly.

Ali saw the fires of rage in his father's eyes and immediately complied by turning the volume on the stereo up to full. Turning back to the man beneath him, Akim opened the pliers and swiftly plunged a single knurled, serrated jaw under the nail of Rashid's left thumb. By then the moaning had become panicked, blood curdling screaming, and Ali's jaw dropped as he saw his father grip the pliers and deftly remove Rashid's thumb nail. He placed the pliers and the thumbnail on the nearby table, and calmly removed a white handkerchief from a pocket under his tunic. The cacophony of terrified screaming and pounding music in the small room seemed to have no effect on Akim as he gently and methodically bound the ragged, bleeding thumb with the handkerchief. Finally, he let go of the raised hand and calmly stared ahead into space as he waited for the howling to stop. It was a minute later when the yelling calmed down to a pitiful sobbing and Akim turned and nodded at Ali who stood spellbound near the stereo. Ali quickly turned the volume of the music down and at the same time his father stood up, dragging Rashid up with him. Using his immense strength, he tossed the limp body back on to the same seat he had sat on only minutes beforehand. The young man sat there shaking violently and clutching his ruined thumb with look of horrified disbelief on his tear covered face. Akim Usmani towered above the terrified man, looked him in the eyes, and spoke.

"Thank you once again for coming to meet us, Rashid" he said calmly "I will be expecting you to return by the end of the week with the full balance owing.."

Rashid nodded frantically as the tears ran down his face.

"Yes, sir.." he whispered "I will bring the money."

"You may leave now.."

The seated man scrambled to his feet and stumbled out of the room hastily with his injured hand clutched to his chest. There followed the thunder of footfalls on the stairs and the slamming of the door as Rashid left the building. Akim Usmani turned and faced his son who still stood flabbergasted near the stereo.

"This is how we deal with debtors, my son" he said calmly "Now, I must go to work."

Ali stared at his father as he made his way towards the door.

"Yes, father.." he said in a shaky voice "Thank you."

Ali Usmani stood there blinking with shock and waited until he heard the yellow door close below. His eyes moved to the table where the pliers and the bloody thumbnail lay. Suddenly a wave of bile rose in his throat and he quickly ran to the bathroom where he was violently sick.

CHAPTER SEVENTEEN

Paranoia

I sat transfixed to the screen of the laptop as I watched and listened to the live proceedings that streamed from the hidden camera in the flat. Although it came as no surprise to finally understand and witness the inner workings of the Usmani family, the sheer speed and clinical brutality of Akim Usmani's assault on the young man had come as a shock. I sat and listened to Ali vomiting in the bathroom until he finally returned to the lounge with a wet dish towel and cleaned up the mess his father had left. The sight of him retching and heaving while attempting to lift the bloody thumb nail from the table top was mildly amusing. The camera automatically turned itself off a minute after he left the flat and I walked to the window with my coffee to think things through. The bright mid morning sunshine lent a rare dab of colour to the grim urban landscape below and I let out a low whistle as I recalled the sudden and ferocious attack on young Rashid. *These are some seriously vile people you're dealing with here, Green. Ruthless and fucking dangerous. A lot of your fears and paranoia are real.* As I stood there staring blankly out of the window I began to attempt to put the facts that I knew to be true into some kind of logical order. First and foremost was the fact that the family were actively involved in the drug trade. Of that there was now no doubt. The fact that the father, Akim, had been involved in the meeting I had just witnessed confirmed that it was no longer just a vice of his son, Ali. It might also explain why there were undercover police watching the factory in South London. The whole thing was turning out to be a lot more complicated than I had initially thought. *But what about the girl? Sharon Pennington.* I lit a cigarette as as I ran through the chronological order of what I had discovered about her. *Well, thanks to Brandon, you now know she's only 15 years old. I think you can pretty much bet on the fact that she's a junkie, and if not, she is most definitely a user. And as to whether she is actually being sexually abused up there in that filthy shit hole of a flat. Well, I think that's a given, Green. And what's more, you'll be able to prove that later tonight. Prove it beyond any doubt. And if so, you might just be able to have the whole lot of them locked up at once. Fuck the insurance fraud. That's minor compared to what they're up to. Won't make much of a difference if they've all been arrested for child abuse and drug dealing would it? Deliver the footage to the police along with addresses and it's a case of job done.* I sipped the coffee as my mind went back to the strange one, Zain Usmani. He was the big unknown.

A puzzling character who seemed somehow distant from his family and their various businesses. A homebody of sorts. To me it seemed that he might be mentally retarded in some way. His unusual dishevelled appearance was in stark contrast to the rest of the men in the family. His skinny frame, the hunched back, and the limp when he walked, all added to this feeling. *But then again, he does drive. He must have a licence. And what about the fertilizer? Ammonium Nitrate. Perhaps it's your paranoia creeping back here, but if you were wrong, the consequences would be appalling. Think, Green, think!* It was as I was walking back to the kitchen to replace the empty coffee mug that I remembered my appointment in South London. I had been totally distracted by the goings on at the flat and then consumed by my thoughts afterwards.

"Shit.." I said out loud as I looked at my watch.

It had just gone 11.00 am and I had arranged to visit the showroom at Akus Trading at midday. *If you leave now you'll make it, Green. Probably a good idea if you take your own vehicle in case those undercover police are still there.*

CHAPTER EIGHTEEN

Brandon Stevens

It was 10.45am when Sharon Pennington arrived at the pharmacy across the street from where Brandon stood. The morning had been quite eventful so far. He had photographed the arrival of Akim and Ali Usmani at the flat above the takeaway earlier and had logged the time and duration of their stay. He had also watched the arrival and rushed departure of the other unknown Asian man. The man had seemed extremely distressed when he left and had run off at speed in the direction of the Islington Angel. Recording everything he had witnessed on his phone, he was certain this flurry of activity would be of interest to Jason, and he decided that this new job wasn't as boring a he had originally thought. Finally things seemed to be moving and Brandon Stevens was actually enjoying himself. Sharon Pennington had first visited the pharmacy across the street emerging some 10 minutes later. She paused in the rare morning sunshine and Brandon took the opportunity to take a clandestine photograph of her with his phone. Wearing her usual puffy pink jacket and tight leggings, she made her way to a nearby cafe and stepped inside. Brandon remembered the instruction from Jason that if there was an opportunity, he should try to strike up another conversation with the girl in order to try to learn a bit more about the Usmani's and the goings on in the flat above the takeaway. 'Keep it casual' he had said. The fact that the girl had entered the cafe was a clear opportunity to do just that, and as soon as there was a gap in traffic he crossed the street. Brandon Stevens felt a wave of excitement as he approached the doors of the cafe. Ever since meeting the girl the previous day, he had been unable to put her out of his mind. Her resemblance to his late sister was uncanny and he had spent a good hour studying her Facebook profile and pictures the previous evening. It was almost as if he felt a duty of care towards the girl. The thought of meeting her again had put a spring in his step and he had to check himself before entering the cafe. *Be calm, act casual.* He told himself repeatedly. Brandon Stevens pushed the door of the cafe open and stepped into the warmth of the shop front. A group of builders in paint splattered overalls sat eating breakfast at a table to his left while a number of other elderly patrons sat alone reading newspapers. He scanned the room until he saw the girl.

She sat alone at the far corner of the cafe, browsing her phone with a steaming mug of tea in front her. Brandon ambled up to the nearby counter and placed an order for a cup of tea and a bacon and egg roll. As he stood there he turned to look at the girl seated to his right. She lifted her gaze from her phone and their eyes met.

"Oh, hello again!" he said with a genuine smile "It's Sharon isn't it?"

"Yeah.." she replied "Brandon, right?"

"Yep...How's it going?"

"Alright I guess, bloody freezing but nice to see some sun.."

"Yeah.." said Brandon with a grin "We ain't gonna see it for a while so best enjoy it while we can! Mind if I join you?"

The girl paused and for a split second there was a slight frown on her forehead. It was almost as if she was suspicious of Brandon's motives and was weighing up her options. Sharon Pennington's short life had been one filled with abuse, exploitation and sadness. Troubled and vulnerable, she was not used to people being nice or friendly to her. But this young man's open smile and cheerful character won her over quickly, and she knew in her heart that he was no threat to her.

"Sure..." she replied with a guarded smile "Why not?"

CHAPTER NINETEEN

South London

It was 11.55 am exactly as I drove into the Stone Industrial Estate in South London to get to my appointment at Akus Trading. I had used my own vehicle in case the undercover police from the previous day were still there watching the premises from their white van. I knew there was a good chance that if they were still there, they would almost certainly recognise me as I entered the facility but that was something I could not avoid. I had spent the 45 minute journey attempting to organize my myriad of thoughts and suspicions into a logical, coherent and actionable order. Although I had learnt a lot, there were still many unanswered questions, some of which were of vital importance. I put them out of my mind as I approached the businesses premises of Akus Trading. The first thing I noticed was the white van which was still parked in the same position it had been the previous day. There were two men sitting in the front seat but I could not see their faces as I drove past and parked near the entrance to the factory. Wasting no time, I climbed out of the vehicle, locked it, and walked towards the front door of the reception with my head turned slightly to the left in the hope that the men in the white van would not recognize me. I pushed the door open and stepped into a large brightly lit room with a tiled shop counter to the rear. Behind it sat a young Asian lady wearing a head scarf. Upon seeing me she stood up and smiled brightly.

"Mr Green?" she said in a cheerful voice.

"That's me.." I said "Are you Samaira?"

"I am.." she replied "Nice to meet you."

I walked up to the counter and shook hands with the young lady. Her pleasant and cheerful manner came as a surprise especially having read in the report that the insurance assessor who had visited previously had been met with unfriendly and uncooperative staff.

If anything, the reception of the business seemed well set out, organized, and pleasant. Behind the counter was a wide sign with the words 'Akus Trading' emblazoned across the front. On the wall to left was a series of large black and white prints showing the firing kilns and ovens in which the tiles were produced. To the right of the area was the showroom with wide display racks of the various tile samples and intricate mosaic patterns set into the concrete floor. To the left of this was another section dedicated to the coffee imports from Kenya. Warm yellow lighting shone down on an impressive display of antique coffee grinders and hessian sacks overflowing with raw coffee beans. The room was filled with the rich aroma of Arabica roast.

"You mentioned you were setting up a restaurant in the city and wanted to look at some tiles?" she said.

"Correct.."

"Well.." she said "Perhaps we can interest you in our coffee as well, but for now please follow me and I'll show you some of our tiles first."

Samaira picked a clip board from behind the counter and we both walked over to the display racks. I spent the next five minutes learning about the origin, history, and manufacturing process of the ceramic tiles from the extremely chatty Samaira. As well as having an extensive knowledge of her products, she was friendly, affable and an extremely good sales person. It was as we were about to move on to the coffee section of the showroom that I heard the front door to the reception opening behind us. I turned around to the see the towering figure of Akim Usmani clutching his briefcase as he strode across the shopfront. Clearly heading towards the access door to the rear of the reception, he paused when he saw us and spoke.

"Good afternoon.." he said.

"Good afternoon, Mr Usmani" said Samaira in her musical voice "This is Mr Green, he's opening a restaurant in London and came to look at our tiles. I was just about to show him our coffee as well.."

Akim Usmani nodded and spoke.

"I see.." he said as he began walking towards us.

The big man approached with a smile on his face that revealed a huge set of perfectly white teeth. He held out his right hand as he arrived. It was only then that I became fully aware of the sheer size of the man. Until then I had only observed him from a distance, but only now, in close proximity, did I realize how big he actually was. At 6 foot 5 inches, his tall wide frame towered above me and for a brief moment it struck me as being somewhat bizarre that I had witnessed the very same person violently rip the thumb nail from another man not hours beforehand. I turned around and shook his hand as he arrived. His hand was cool and dry but his powerful fingers gripped my own like a vice, and I realized then that this was a man of formidable strength.

"Jason Green.." I said casually "Pleased to meet you."

"Thank you for coming, Mr Green" he said in his familiar deep voice "My name is Akim Usmani. I hope Samaira has been looking after you?"

"Yes.." I said turning once again to the tiles "She's been very helpful. In fact I think I'm going to instruct my architect to come down here and take a look with a view to using your tiles in the restaurant. They are very beautiful."

"Excellent.." came the reply "And did you have a chance to try our coffee?"

"Not yet.."

"Ah, well in that case please come through to my office and have a cup. Ours is a particularly fine strain of Arabica, straight from the highlands of Kenya.."

"Sure.." I said glancing at my watch "I have some time, why not?"

"Excellent.." he said turning to the girl "Samaira, would you please bring two cups of our finest blend to my office. Mr Green, please, follow me."

Akim Usmani's grey tunic billowed behind him as I followed him through the access door and down a long corridor to his office. I was ushered in and offered a comfortable seat near an expansive desk. The room was decorated with paintings of mountain scenes from what I imagined must have been his native Pakistan, while behind the desk was a window that looked into the warehouse bay itself. I noticed a couple of forklifts and pallets of ceramic tiles stacked up to the beams of the building with an equally large stack of hessian sacks of coffee beans nearby.

"Now, Mr Green" said Usmani as he took his seat behind the desk "Were you given any pamphlets or price lists for the tile selection?"

"Not yet, no.."

"Well.." he said as he opened his briefcase "I have some here which I can give you now."

I watched as he rummaged in the briefcase eventually retrieving a set of glossy pamphlets. He reached over the wide desk and handed them to me. It was at that moment that I saw a flicker of fire in his dark piercing eyes. It was almost as if he had seen through my ruse and had somehow become suspicious of my motives. The moment was broken by the arrival of Samaira who carried a tray with two small cups on it. With a wide smile on her face she handed one to me and the other to Usmani.

"Enjoy!" she said before leaving the room.

The coffee was excellent and the next few minutes were spent making small talk about its superior qualities. It was when I had almost finished my cup that he spoke once again.

"Perhaps I can offer you a sample pack of our coffee Mr Green?" he said "As you are in the restaurant business, it might be of interest."

"Sure.." I said placing the empty cup on the desk "Thanks very much. I'll give it to the chef this afternoon and see what he thinks"

Akim Usmani stood up and walked to a display cabinet on the wall to the right. He opened the door and peered inside.

"Hmm" he said "It appears Samaira forgot to restock my samples. I will need to go into the warehouse briefly to collect one. Two minutes Mr Green.."

"No problem.." I said sitting back in my seat "Thanks very much."

I watched as the big man left the room and turned left to enter the warehouse. It was only then that I remembered the pouch of surveillance equipment in my jacket pocket. It had been there since the previous night when I had entered the flat above the takeaway with the cameras. I knew there was a miniature tracking device in there and all that was needed to activate it was to pull the seal from the unit. I quickly felt my left breast pocket to confirm it was still there. It was. I looked around the room for anything I might be able to place it in. *The briefcase, Green. He is never without it. It has to be the briefcase!* I stood up from my seat and looked through the window to the warehouse beyond. Akim Usmani was making his way over towards the stack of coffee to the left. *If you're gonna do it Green, you'd better be quick!* I reached into my pocket and pulled out the small leather pouch. After unzipping it I grabbed the tiny Japanese device and ripped the seal from the one sided tape. Weighing only 24 grams and no bigger than a coin, the thin black unit had a battery life of two weeks when activated and sent out real time tracking information every five seconds. Added to these impressive features was the fact that the unit was not limited by distance and would function literally anywhere on the globe. Keeping my eye on the warehouse, I leant forward and turned the open briefcase towards me in order to access it. As expected, it was full of papers and pamphlets but it was the the thin rear compartments that interested me. Using my left hand, I pulled at the steel fasteners of the back compartment. They opened easily and the compartment hung open revealing nothing but a few forgotten sheets of paper. I placed the tracking device as far out of sight as possible at the bottom right of the case and pressed it into place to ensure it would stay put. It was at that moment that I saw Akim Usmani returning. Carrying a small gold packet of coffee in his hand, he was making his way swiftly out of the warehouse area and back to the office. *Shit! Hurry up Green!*

I ducked down quickly to avoid him seeing me through the window and quickly clipped the rear compartment of the briefcase in place. Once done, I pushed it back to where he had left it on the desk. Keeping my body low to the desk, I sat back on the chair a split second before he returned and walked in behind me.

"Now then, Mr Green" he said handing me the packet "Here is your sample of coffee and I sincerely hope we can do business.."

"Thank you Mr Usmani" I said as I stood up "You are very kind, I'm certain we will."

With the pamphlets and the coffee in hand I followed the big man out into the reception area. I stopped briefly to shake his hand and say goodbye to Samaira and left the the building. The freezing air outside came as a shock and I glanced quickly at the white van parked 50 metres away to my left. The figures of the two men were still seated in the front. Without pausing I unlocked the vehicle, climbed in and drove off.

CHAPTER TWENTY

Zain Usmani

Zain Usmani groaned quietly as he stood up from his kneeling position on the prayer mat. His hunched back was aching more than usual and his eyes were bloodshot from fatigue and exposure to chemical fumes. It had been more than 24 hours since he had last slept and although his mother had delivered his meals as usual, he had eaten very little. The chemical processes of isolating and separating the Ammonium Nitrate powder from the fertiliser had been complicated and tedious. It had involved a constant system of heating, blending, boiling, and drying the various liquid solutions. The extractor fan had been essential during this process as the pungent fumes from the Bunsen burners and the bubbling round bottom flasks were highly toxic. But although he was physically exhausted, Zain Usmani was feeling elated. To the right hand side of his work bench stood five flasks of pure white Ammonium Nitrate powder. The by product of this process was a pile of small brown crystalline chunks which lay in a sealed plastic bag nearby. The next step was to safely dispose of the waste product and to collect 5 litres of diesel fuel. He opened his cupboard and removed a fake Adidas rucksack in which he placed the small bag of waste crystals and an empty 5 litre plastic jerry can. He quickly donned his thick winter jacket and slung the rucksack over his right shoulder. It was as he was in the process of unlocking his door that he paused and turned to look at the fruits of his labour on the work bench behind him. He cast his eye proudly over the piles of equipment and tools he had acquired then glanced at the black flag of the Islamic State that hung in pride of place above his bed.

"Allahu Akbar" he whispered to himself.

The short walk up the street and around the corner to the service station took only 15 minutes. He used this excursion to dump the bag of waste crystals in rubbish bin near a building site. Using cash, he purchased 5 litres of diesel from the service station then placed the jerry can in the rucksack. He knew that if he were to be seen carrying the container by a family member it would raise questions and this was something he had to avoid. It was 20 minutes later when Zain Usmani finally stepped into his room and locked the door behind him. Placing the jerry can on the work bench, he sat down and prepared to get to work once again.

Reaching under the bench, he lifted the sack of fireworks he had purchased and placed it in front of him. Now would be the process of de-constructing them and removing the fuse components from them all. It would involve a process of dissecting and scraping each of them in order to separate the tiny amounts of incendiary powder he needed. Then would be the process of refining that powder and packing it into a series of hollowed out torch batteries. These would then be sealed with a fast setting putty effectively creating a series of home made capped fuses capable of setting off the main explosive charge. The capped fuses would be suspended inside the empty cannister of refrigeration gas, and the cannister then tightly packed with the Ammonium

Nitrate and diesel mixture. The fuses themselves would then be wired to the battery and the simple mechanical oven timer, leaving only the last job which would be to strap the heavy bags of steel bolts and nails to the outside of the cannister. He had learned from the online tutorials on the dark web that these final preparations would be by far the most dangerous part of the process. Zain Usmani was worn down and weary but at the same time he was filled with an impassioned and fanatical religious fervour. His grand plan would be carried out that very night. The city would be shaken to its core and London would never be the same again. He blinked his bloodshot eyes as he stared at the nearly completed project in front of him.

"Alamdulilliah.." he whispered quietly to himself. 'All praise is due to God alone'.

CHAPTER TWENTY ONE

Brandon Stevens

Brandon Stevens and Sharon Pennington laughed heartily as they made their way up the street towards Highbury Park. They had spent the past 90 minutes chatting in the cafe and Brandon had bought her a full English breakfast. Although he was acutely aware that this was a professional assignment, he found himself enjoying the girl's company and had succeeded in breaking down her barriers to the point where he felt like they had known each other for years. For him it was a fond, brotherly affection not least brought on by the striking physical similarities she had to his late sister. But it was not only that. There was also her sense of humour which he had managed to unearth and his jokes had brought this out to the point where he realized that she was funny and smart to boot. It was as they reached the turn off to the high rise housing estate that Sharon Pennington paused and the smile disappeared from her face.

"What's wrong?" asked Brandon with genuine concern.

"Nothing.." she replied sadly "I just don't feel like going home right now."

"Well.." said Brandon cheerfully "It's a sunny day, we're having a laugh, why don't we go sit in the sun in park for a while?"

"Yeah?" came the reply "What about your job? Don't you need to get back?"

"Nah..." said Brandon blithely "I can take a couple of hours off. Come on, let's go! It's a gorgeous sunny day!"

Sharon Pennington gazed wistfully down the hill towards the bleak high rise blocks then turned to Brandon once again.

"Yeah.." she said as her face lit up once again "Let's do that."

The unlikely couple crossed the street and made their way down the boundary of the park and in through one of the many entrances.

Although the sun was out, it was still cold enough to ensure that there were very few people in the area apart from the odd dog walker. They took a seat on a bench in a sunny spot and continued their jovial conversation. Sharon Pennington felt comfortably at ease and laughed constantly at Brandon's quick Cockney wit and charm. To anyone passing, the two of them simply looked like a pair of siblings or friends catching up after some time apart. But it was half an hour later, during a lull in the conversation that the atmosphere suddenly changed. The years of drug taking and physical abuse had resulted in Sharon Pennington naturally assuming and wrongly interpreting any form of male attention as being sexually motivated. She turned and stared at Brandon with a glazed look in her eyes and casually placed her left hand on his leg. Taken completely by surprise, Brandon Stevens was rendered speechless and stared down in horror as she slowly moved her hand up towards his groin.

"What are you doing?" he shouted out loud as he gripped her forcefully by the wrist.

In doing this he accidentally pulled the sleeve of the puffy pink jacket up to reveal the young girl's forearm. There, in full view, were a series of parallel scars, some of them still scabbed and new.

"What the fuck is this?" he shouted, pointing at the scarred flesh "Who did this to you?"

Sharon Pennington's face was a picture of shock and confusion and her eyes instantly welled up with tears.

"I'm sorry, Brandon.." she said in a trembling voice "I thought..."

"Who cut you like that? Who did this?" he shouted.

"I did.." she sobbed as she pulled her arm away "I do it to myself!"

This unexpected moment was a turning point in the relationship between Brandon Stevens and Sharon Pennington.

Her tears came in great heaving sobs as she recounted the daily horrors of her life of abuse and exploitation. Acutely upset himself at seeing the anguish of the young girl, Brandon put a brotherly arm around her shoulder and comforted her as he coaxed and encouraged her to talk openly. This kind and protective gesture from Brandon earned him her trust and after the initial bout of weeping, she began the long process of telling him everything. Sharon Pennington had been self harming for the past 18 months. It had started when her single mother had met her new boyfriend and invited him into their home. A violent alcoholic, he had started sexually abusing her soon after moving in, and this had continued to the present day. This abuse had initially caused her to suffer from low self esteem and a sense of isolation and worthlessness. She had found some twisted form of solace in cutting her arms repeatedly with a razor blade she kept in a drawer in her room. Having already come from a broken home and now being faced with constant abuse in the only place she had ever felt safe, Sharon Pennington had found herself on the streets and in an extremely vulnerable position. It had been then that she had met Ali Usmani who had introduced her to heroin and groomed her into prostitution. The vice like grip of the drug had ensured his control over her was complete and she had been visiting the flat above the takeaway every night for the past year. Brandon sat and listened in horror as she recounted the physical and mental abuse she had suffered at the hands of the men who frequented the flat. But at the same time, he came to understand that this was all she knew. Without realizing it, his protective brotherly instincts were kicking in and he knew then he had to put a stop to it all. With her make up spoiled and mascara running down her chubby cheeks, she was a pitiful sight, and Brandon comforted her quietly while deep down inside his anger boiled. In his mind he had already decided that there was no way he would allow this to continue. He had no idea that this was something that would very soon place both of their lives in grave danger.

"Don't worry.." he said quietly as he rubbed her shoulder "I'm gonna help you."

CHAPTER TWENTY TWO

Green

It was 3.25 pm by the time I made it back to my flat in North London. The traffic had been heavy and I had been completely preoccupied by the many jumbled thoughts that cluttered my mind. The strange juxtaposition between the explosive violence I had witnessed from Akim Usmani on the hidden camera earlier to the apparently mild mannered businessman I had just met was stark and surprising. *How can someone go from one extreme to another so effortlessly?* But that was just one of many thoughts and questions that needed answering. I put them all out of my mind as I turned the kettle on and called Brandon.

"Hello mate, how are you?" I said as he answered.

"Oh, hi Jason, yeah, I'm alright.." he replied sounding somewhat vague "Not a lot to report I'm afraid"

"What about the girl, Sharon. You've not seen her? Nothing else at all?"

"Nah.." he replied "Nah it's been pretty quiet around here"

"Well, if anything interesting happens let me know. If not, I'll see you tomorrow morning at my flat, same time.."

"Yeah..Of course.." he replied "Yeah, I'll see you then"

I frowned as I hung up the phone feeling somewhat puzzled by Brandon's change in attitude. *Who knows Green, he's young.* Picking up the sample pack of Kenyan coffee I had been given by Usmani, I went into the kitchen to make a cup. It smelt good when I put it in the French press and I carried the open packet with me to my my desk as I let it brew. The first thing I did was to log onto the website of the tracking device. The plastic seal I had ripped from the device when I had planted it had a unique 10 digit serial number printed on it. It was this number that identified the specific device and I typed the number into the search bar on the website and waited for it to boot up. I drummed my fingers impatiently on the desk as I waited for the technology to kick in.

Eventually the screen opened to show a detailed map of London with a small blue dot that pulsed in the centre. Akim Usmani was on the move heading North, more than likely heading back home. *Well, it's working. Good.* I walked back into the kitchen and pressed the plunger on the French press. The coffee was dark and rich and I carried the steaming cup back to my computer. The sample packet of coffee was gold in colour and I turned it in my hand as I studied it. It came as a surprise to see it had been packed in Kenya by a company by the name of none other than Akus Trading based in the town of Kutus, in the Kirinyaga area some 120 km North of the capital, Nairobi. *Well, well, Mr Usmani. Your wings are well spread.* A quick google search showed there was no official website for the packing company and all searches led to the same website I had visited while sitting outside the

London warehouse. I took a deep breath as I sat back and sipped the coffee. *This has to come to an end Green.* I stood up and walked over to the bay windows to smoke and think. The late afternoon sun was waning, leaving the bleak urban landscape below shadowed and dingy looking. *You've got enough, Green. The video evidence you have already will suffice. Then of course there'll be whatever is recorded in the bedroom of that filthy shit hole flat tonight. That'll be the cherry on the cake for sure. Akim, Ali, maybe all of them, who knows? The police will certainly take a very keen interest in what you have so far. Then there's the fact that they're already watching the factory. No, Green, these are some seriously vile human beings you're dealing with here...This will all end, and it will end tomorrow.*

CHAPTER TWENTY THREE

Zain Usmani

Zain Usmani grunted as he strapped the last of the heavy plastic bags of steel nails to the side of the refrigeration gas cannister. He had spent the afternoon sealing the batteries that made up the capped fuses and packing the freon cannister with the toxic Ammonium Nitrate and diesel mixture. After connecting the wiring to the battery and the oven timer, he had sealed the top of the cannister with some fast setting putty. Eventually he stood back and blinked his stinging eyes as he admired the fruits of his labour. The addition of the bags of steel bolts and nails had caused the device to appear crude and unwieldy what with the multiple layers of duct tape, but there was absolutely no doubt in his mind that he had created something that was capable of killing hundreds.

"Allahu Akbar.." he whispered to himself "They'll have to scrape them off the walls."

Buzzing with a mixture of extreme fatigue and pure adrenalin, he stepped forward to conduct one final check on the device. Five minutes later, having found no faults, he removed his traditional grey tunic and began dressing in the flashy Western clothes he had chosen to wear for the occasion. Of course the tunic would go back on over these clothes as he left the house, but this would be removed once he had entered the underground system. His intention was to appear as much like any other infidel as possible so as not to attract any unwanted attention. He would enter Victoria Station, head upstairs to the Weatherspoons pub, activate the timer and place the rucksack at the prearranged spot. He had been through this meticulously prepared plan a thousand times in his mind but now, finally, his moment of glory had arrived. *Tonight the very fires of Hell will burn in the city of London and Zain Usmani will make his mark in this world. Allahu Akbar.* A thousand thoughts raced through his mind as he sat on the dirty unmade bed and tied the laces of the brand new trainers he bought especially for the occasion. *Every warrior has fears*. He thought. *Every warrior has doubts. Remember the scriptures of the Qur'an. Be guided by the spirit of Ali ibn Abi Talib and the prophet Muhammad, peace be upon him. Fear nothing. Victory is yours!* Finally, Zain Usmani stood and examined himself in the full length mirror in the corner of the room. On thousands of previous occasions he had stood and done exactly the same thing.

But before it had always been to lament and bemoan his own deeply flawed physical appearance and attributes. This time, however, it was different and he stared at himself with a simmering pride and admiration. Although he wore the gaudy and offensive clothes of the infidels, his was a higher mission. A calling from God himself. Still staring at himself in the mirror, he pulled his grey tunic over the new clothes and donned his thick blue jacket. Next he removed the fake Adidas rucksack from the cupboard and placed it on the work bench next to the bomb. Slowly and carefully, he lifted the heavy, cumbersome device and placed in in the rucksack. Zain Usmani turned and took two small pillows from the top of the cupboard. These would be packed on either side of the device and would act as stabilisers to keep it upright and secure during the journey to the city. It was five minutes later when Zain Usmani fastened the top of the rucksack and stood back to take a look at it. His mouth was dry with fear and excitement and he pulled a packet of chewing gum from his pocket. His hand trembled as he put the gum in his mouth and began chewing furiously. He glanced at the black flag of the Islamic State above his bed and then back to the rucksack on the work bench.

"It is time.." he whispered "Allahu Akbar"

CHAPTER TWENTY FOUR

Confrontation

The rain fell heavily and pattered on the bay windows as I stared out into the darkness below. The weather report had announced there would be gale force winds along with a Siberian cold front expected for the next 4 days. I had spent the past three hours debating on how best to present my evidence on the Usmani's to the police the following morning. The events of the previous days had left a foul taste in my mouth and I had decided that the sooner I put an end to it all, the better. I had resolved to be as open as possible with the police and give them full disclosure as to the reasons I had been watching them. I was, after all, a licenced private investigator and surveillance was part of my daily work. The photographic and video evidence I had on them already would ensure the Usmani's would go down for the drugs. Then, of course, there would be the recordings of whatever transpired in the flat that night. I had grappled with the very knowledge of it and my urge to stop it, but had eventually decided that it had been going on for some time, and if I could produce actual video evidence of sexual abuse on a minor, it would ensure even more lengthy prison sentences for those involved. *It's a tough one, Green. But it'll be worth it in the end.* Along with the sordid scum that was the Usmani family I had been watching, the winter in the city was beginning to get me down and could feel the familiar dark waves of depression advancing. I had long suffered from seasonal affective disorder, or SAD, and this winter was proving to be no different. Soon the familiar cycle of work, excess alcohol and bad food would begin again and carry on through until Spring. I had promised myself each year to avoid it, to fight it and concentrate on exercise and maybe take a break somewhere sunny. I turned around and looked at the laptop on the desk. Soon the cameras in the flat above the takeaway would activate and begin streaming and recording. The thought of what I might witness further turned my stomach and I found myself glancing at the nearby liquor cabinet. *Maybe a drink will help? Just one or two. It's not gonna be easy to watch, Green.* Quietly cursing to myself I turned back to stare out at the darkness beyond the windows. *Fuck that, Green. There's no way you're going to sit here torturing yourself watching that and drinking alone. Plus there's no dinner here. No, you need to get out.* I took my phone out of my pocket and summoned an Uber cab.

Let the cameras do their job and record whatever goes on. Spare yourself the misery of witnessing it. Then tomorrow you hand everything in to the police and be done with it. Wash your hands of it and move on. The wind howled through the dark streets and the rain blew sideways as I waited for the cab under the overhang at the entrance to my block. Thankfully it arrived soon after and I quickly climbed into the back and told the driver to take me to Highbury. The drive took 15 minutes and eventually I walked into the familiar warmth and comfort of The Queen's Head Pub. As he had done the previous night, the barman started pulling my pint before I got to the bar. The atrocious weather had ensured there were only a few regulars in the house and I took my usual seat near the window with a clear view of Supreme Kebabs across the street. I drank a full half pint as I stared at the building knowing full well the depravity that took place within its walls. It was half an hour later when Sharon Pennington arrived and stood at the yellow door waiting to be let in. Like clockwork, Ali Usmani appeared from the rear of the takeaway soon after and opened the door. As before, the lights in the upstairs flat went on and glowed a dull red through the dirty curtains. I walked back to the bar to order my third pint.

"I'll have a double Scotch as well please.." I said to the barman.

The portly man sensed my unease and raised his left eyebrow at my order. I drank the whisky in one swallow at the bar and returned to my seat with the pint. I was on my fourth pint and my appetite was gone by the time the first man arrived. I recognized him from the previous nights although he wore a thick waterproof jacket to shield him against the rain. By then my mood was dark and my thoughts beginning to swim from the alcohol. It was probably a sense of helplessness at what I knew to be happening in the flat across the road. I turned in my seat and nodded at the barman to order a fresh pint. *Don't stress, Green. This will all be over soon.* It was a full hour later when Akim Usmani arrived. He parked his Volvo station wagon in the alleyway behind his son's BMW and headed upstairs. I shook my head in disgust as I stood up to walk outside for a cigarette. It was as I was standing in the shelter of the awning lighting the cigarette that I saw Brandon. He approached on foot on the far side of the street from the right.

His hair was soaking wet as were his clothes and he strode with purpose past the convenience shop and up to the yellow door. I stood there in the darkness, frozen as I watched. *What the hell is going on?*

What the fuck are you doing, Brandon? Clearly upset, the young man stepped up to the door and began pounding on it repeatedly with his right fist. Through the roar of the wind and the noise from the passing traffic I could hear him.

"Sharon!" he shouted between blows.

Unable to move, I stood and watched as he stepped back from the door and looked up at the windows above.

"Sharon, come down from there!" he screamed.

With the cigarette still hanging from my lips I watched as he walked back up to the door and began pounding on it once again.

"Sharon!" he cried "Come down here now!"

It was as I was about to run across the street to stop him that the yellow door opened and Akim Usmani stormed out. He immediately grabbed Brandon by his collar and began forcing him back past the kebab shop towards the alleyway. At that moment Ali Usmani emerged from the takeaway and joined his father in forcing the hapless young man back. The shouting from the chaotic scuffle was muffled by the howling of the wind and it was clear that the sheer size and strength of Akim was no match for young Brandon. The three men quickly disappeared into the alleyway and I had to fight the urge to run across to help Brandon. I quickly moved to the left to get a better view while staying in the darkness of the awning above. In the gloom I saw that Brandon was now lying on the cobbles and both Ali and his father were busy giving him a good kicking. *Fuck that. You cannot allow this, Green.* I ran forward to cross the street but as I arrived at the kerbside a black cab drove past spraying me with freezing, dirty water. At the same time a large truck blocked my view on the far side of the street and I stood unable to move until it passed.

When finally it did, I saw both Akim and Ali walking back towards the takeaway with no Brandon in sight. Clearly having a heated conversation, the two men both entered the yellow door and disappeared upstairs. The entire episode had taken place in the space of less than a minute. At that moment Brandon emerged from the alleyway looking like a drowned rat and rubbing the side of his face. He stumbled off dejectedly to the left heading towards Finsbury Park. Seeing a gap in the traffic, I ran across the road through the driving rain to confront him and reached him some 20 seconds later. I pulled him around by his shoulder to see he was weeping and his right eye already beginning to swell up from the beating. It was a truly pitiful sight.

"Brandon.." I shouted "What were you thinking? You're jeopardising everything!"

"She told me, Jason!" he spluttered "She told me everything. The drugs, and what those people do to her. I had to try and stop it..I had to!"

Seeing he was extremely upset and more than likely in a state of shock, I pulled him gently by his right arm in order to guide him across the road and into the dry and warmth of the pub.

"Come with me" I said "Let's get out of this rain.."

CHAPTER TWENTY FIVE

Zain Usmani

The wet, frigid night air did nothing to stop Zain Usmani sweating as he waited under the blue lights of the Bureau De Change on Elbury Street. His entire body trembled with a mixture of raw fear and religious fervour. As he stared at his cheap digital watch he mumbled to himself repeatedly.

"Allahu Akbar, Allahu Akbar.."

It had been exactly 7 minutes since he had set the timer and activated the bomb. The drunken, fornicating infidels had no idea what was about to happen. The very fires of Hell were about to pay a courtesy call on Victoria Station. In his mind he pictured the shredded bodies of the dead. The bloodied injured and the dying in amongst the twisted wreckage and the flames. In his ears he heard the screams of the maimed, the sirens and the chaos. Zain Usmani's moment of glory was only minutes away and his body was vibrating in anticipation of hearing the blast of the bomb he himself had created. A number of pedestrians glanced at him as they passed but quickly decided that the strange looking man must be mentally retarded and quickly moved on. The seconds felt like minutes, and the minutes like hours as he waited breathlessly with his eyes transfixed on his watch. But the seconds and minutes passed and nothing changed. There was no ground shaking boom from the nearby station. No bright fiery glow in the sky above. No wailing sirens or screaming people. Nothing. Zain Usmani told himself the moment would arrive any at second. That perhaps it was simply a delay on the oven timer. But the minutes passed and all he heard was the sound of the traffic and the wind howling in the streets. Gradually his raging religious fervour began to be replaced by a deeply sullen sense of failure. A dreadful acceptance that nothing he ever did was a success. Perhaps his father was right after all and he was simply a useless, dirty retard? It was a full half hour later when a humiliated, frozen and depressed Zain Usmani decided to return to the station. By then he had convinced himself that there must have been a simple technical error that had caused the device to fail. With his head hung low he limped through the wet streets solemnly until he reached the entrance to the grand old building. Although the concourse was noisy and packed with people it seemed somehow surreal and silent to him. It was with a feeling of deep sadness and shame that he stepped onto the escalator that led to the upper level where the pub was located.

The carol singing children were gone leaving only the drunken infidels above. It was as he entered the pub that his hearing seemed to return and their raucous laughter and shouting seemed to taunt him. It was as if they were all celebrating his failure. The noise of it grew louder and louder in his brain until it felt like he was drowning in a swirling ocean of sin and evil. By the time Zain Usmani reached the barrel table at the far side of the pub he was shaking and whimpering softly. He reached down and lifted the fake Adidas bag that held the bomb and as he walked out of the back doors he strapped it to his back once again. The weight of it caused his hunched back to ache deeply and tears of anger and disappointment filled his eyes. Three minutes later a very dejected Zain Usmani descended into the warmth of the underground to catch a train home.

CHAPTER TWENTY SIX

Confessions

"Sit here" I said to Brandon when we finally walked back into the pub and got to my table.

The young man was trembling with anger and his right eye was swelling heavily. I walked up to the barman who had missed the commotion on the other side of the street and ordered a double whisky.

"Drink this, it'll warm you up.." I said as I took my seat "Now, tell me what's going on mate? Why did you do that?"

Brandon Stevens sat staring out of the window at the red curtains of the flat above the takeaway. I could only assume that his vague attitude during our conversation earlier had something to do with it. He lifted the whisky glass with both and hands and took a sip from it. Finally he took his eyes from the window and looked at me.

"She told me everything, Jason..." he said "You won't believe it."

Oh I will. I thought ruefully. *I will*. I spent the next 30 minutes listening to the young man as he recounted what he had learnt from the girl. Although I already knew a lot of it, I chose to remain quiet and allow him to him speak. He told me of the abuse she was suffering and how their unlikely friendship had formed. He told me of his late sister who bore a striking resemblance to her as well. He told me that the father, Akim, was a major drug dealer who was much feared in the community. Again, these were things I already knew but I chose to remain quiet and let him offload. By the time he had finished talking he had calmed down but his eye was swollen and turning a dark shade of purple. I knew then I had to tell the young man about my plans with the police, but I decided not to mention the cameras I had placed in the flat.

"Listen to me, Brandon" I said "I know what you're telling me is true. I know what's going on here, and I want you to know that this will all be over tomorrow. I have enough evidence on this family to hammer them properly.

We will be taking our findings to the police in the morning and they will all be arrested. Simple as that. It ends tomorrow, don't worry."

The young man looked at me with a slightly puzzled expression on his face. I pulled my phone from my pocket and summoned an Uber cab.

"The best thing we can do now is to go home and get some rest" I said. "You be at my flat at 9.00 am tomorrow and you and I will put a stop to all of this."

"Okay, Jason.." he replied sullenly.

The drive to my flat took only 10 minutes and I handed the driver some extra money for the ongoing journey to Brandon's house.

"I'll see you tomorrow.." I said to Brandon as I got out of the vehicle "Don't worry about a thing."

I dashed through the freezing rain into the block and headed up to the 5th floor. By then the alcohol had long since worn off leaving me feeling dehydrated and slightly ill. The first thing I did was to check the hidden cameras in the flat. Both had recorded activity but as expected it was the one in the bedroom that had the most. I had no intention of watching either but I needed to be certain that what had been recorded was what I expected. The footage did not disappoint and what I saw in the brief clip I did watch made me sick to my stomach. I immediately closed my laptop and headed for a long hot shower. Once again I felt the urge to scrub my body from the filth I had witnessed and rid myself of the whole sordid affair. Eventually I lay on my bed and stared at the ceiling as I planned my next move. I decided that I would present the photographic and video evidence of the drugs and the sexual abuse on a flash stick. I would also give a detailed statement and get Brandon to do the same. Presented with such overwhelming evidence, the police would have no choice but to act and act quickly.

They'll all be behind bars by the afternoon, Green. No doubt about that. I lay there on the bed for a good 20 minutes playing the events of the past few days over and over in my mind until eventually I drifted off to a troubled and restless sleep.

CHAPTER TWENTY SEVEN

The Missing

It was 7.00 am when I woke up. My mouth was dry and I reached for the glass of water on the bedside. I had two hours before Brandon was due to arrive and I decided that I would use that time copying photographs and video files onto a flash stick and preparing for our visit to the police station. Once he arrived I would give him a run down of everything I knew, telling him about the videos I had recorded as well. Once he was fully briefed, we would both head to Finsbury Park police station and make our reports. Given the amount of evidence I already had, I assumed we would be there for at least a couple of hours and I felt certain they would make arrests immediately. I had a dull headache as I walked through to the kitchen to boil the kettle for coffee. It was still dark when I drew the curtains open and saw the rain was still falling. I stood there staring out into the darkness and smoked my first cigarette of the day. *Well, there's one good thing, Green. You got some decent coffee out of the whole shit show.* I turned on the television news and sat down to get to work transferring the video and photo files onto a spare flash stick. I would add any more that Brandon had on his phone before we left for the police station. It was 8.00 am by the time I headed for a shower and shave then dressed for the day and cooked a small breakfast. The daylight was starting to cast a pale grey glow on the horizon by 9.00 am and I was anxious to get moving. I glanced at my watch as I sipped my second cup of coffee. *Where's Brandon?* I thought. *He's running late, not like him.* Then I recalled the state he was in the previous evening and the beating he had received. *Give him a bit of time, he was very upset last night.* I paced the room for another five minutes growing more and more impatient. Finally I picked up my phone and rang his number. There was no reply and eventually the call went to voice mail. Seeing no point in pacing the room I sat down and turned the volume up on the news. The weather report was on, telling of damage from the storm the previous night. I sat there drumming my fingers impatiently on the sofa as I waited. It was at 9.30 am, and many unanswered calls later when I decided to head off alone.

Wrapping up warm, I left my flat and headed downstairs to the parked hire car. The wind was still blowing the rain sideways and the real feel of the early daylight temperature was below freezing. I made a dash through the rain to the car from the shelter of the overhang and quickly climbed in. With the engine running I sat and waited for the interior to warm up. All the while I kept an eye on the rear view mirror in case Brandon arrived. He never did. Before leaving I made one final call to his phone which still went unanswered. *Strange. What the hell could he be doing?* The main road up to Highbury was littered with twigs and small branches from the previous night's storm and I was surprised to see Ali's BMW parked in the alleyway at Supreme Kebabs and the flat as I passed. I shook my head as I drove past and decided I would ask the police to retrieve and return my surveillance cameras once they had completed their investigations. It was as I was approaching the busy junction at Finsbury Park that I decided to give Brandon a final call. *Give him one more chance Green he might be on his way.* The traffic was heavy so I made a right turn and headed back to street where the Usmani house was. It turned out the only parking space was the one I had used on the previous days while watching the house. I pulled in and turned the engine off. I immediately noticed Akim Usmani's Volvo was not parked in its usual spot. *Must be at the warehouse.* The grey pebble dash facade was wet and grim looking and as usual the doors and windows were closed. It was as I was about to call Brandon one final time that I felt the urge for a cigarette. *Christ.* I thought. *You're not supposed to smoke in the hired car.* There was a lull in the rain so I stepped out of the vehicle to smoke. With no reply and the call once again going voicemail, I pocketed the phone and pulled the pack of cigarettes from my pocket. It was as I was lighting the cigarette that I saw the curtains of the upstairs window open and a shadow of human movement beyond the extractor fan.

CHAPTER TWENTY EIGHT

Bang

Zain Usmani awoke at around 9.30 am with a runny nose and a mild headache. He had always been somewhat unhealthy and susceptible to colds and flu and he was convinced that the prolonged period of being outdoors in the wet and cold the previous night had caused this. He lay in his bed in the gloomy darkness of his upstairs room and recalled the sad and disappointing events of the previous evening. He felt humiliated and ashamed that his grand plan had failed and he had been forced to return home carrying the device he had worked so hard to create. Reaching down below his bed, he lifted a roll of toilet paper, tore off a strip, and blew his nose weakly. He tossed the used tissue onto the large pile of the same near his bed and fluffed his stained pillow up so he could lie there and examine his work bench. The unwieldy and bulbous device sat there where he had left it. He had been too tired and upset to examine it when he had eventually returned home last night. *What could have gone wrong?* He thought. *I followed everything precisely and did exactly what I was instructed to do.* He lay there going through it all in his mind for the next 15 minutes until he had a thought. *It has to have been a fault with the electrical circuit. There's absolutely nothing else that could have gone wrong.* In his mind he went through the simple circuit again and again until he had convinced himself beyond any doubt. *I can fix this! My grand plan will go ahead! Alhamdulillah!* Zain Usmani lifted the dirty yellow duvet cover and sat up on the side of his bed. His hunched back ached as he stood, and wearing nothing but his underwear, he walked over to the crude home made bomb that sat on the bench. He bent over and examined the wiring atop the device but the room was too dark to allow this to be done efficiently. He pulled the string to turn on the overhead light and reached over and opened the curtains. As he did this he had no idea he was being watched by a man smoking a cigarette on the street not far away. Zain Usmani pulled his work chair over and sat down to get to work. Almost immediately he had a revelation. One of the tiny wires that made up the main circuit from the lead acid battery had indeed come loose. There it was, as plain as day, right there in front of him. A sudden wave of relief swept over him and a smile formed on his face as a dribble of mucous ran from his right nostril into his moustache.

"I knew it!" he whispered excitedly.

But it was this sudden enthusiasm that caused Zain Usmani to make his fatal mistake. He had forgotten that the simple oven timer was set to zero and the entire circuit system was live and still connected to the lead acid battery. With his right hand he reached down and grabbed the loose wire. As he did this there came a knock on the door.

"Sabah alkhyr ya waladia. laqad 'ahdarat alfatur walshaay" said his mother from behind the locked door. 'Good morning my son. I have brought your breakfast and tea.'

"Ana mashghulat, 'umi!" he replied impatiently 'I'm busy, Mother!'

At that moment, Zain Usmani plunged the exposed wire into the tiny socket it should have been in all along. As he did so there was a tiny, almost invisible electrical spark.

The explosion was colossal and blinding in its intensity. It shook the ground and rattled the foundations of the entire block. The roof of the Usmani house was blown to pieces with tiles, shrapnel and blockwork launched hundreds of feet into the air above. It blew away the floors on both levels below, cracking and distorting the brickwork of the house. Every window was blown outwards in a thousand tinkling chunks of double glazing. Both Zain Usmani and his long suffering mother were instantly vaporized, later only identified by their DNA. The destruction was instant and complete, and a huge fireball rose hundreds of feet into the sky followed by a dark billowing mushroom cloud of noxious fumes. Not even the light rain that started falling immediately afterwards could quell the raging inferno that burnt in what was left of the Usmani home. Surrounding houses had their windows blown in while the nearby street was littered with broken bricks and chunks of smoking wooden roof beams. The sky above darkened and as the flames roared, the rain brought down a layer of grey ash that settled lightly on every surface within a hundred metre radius.

CHAPTER TWENTY NINE

Akim Usmani

Akim Usmani sat relaxed on his sumptuous chair in his office at the South London warehouse of Akus Trading. The time was 10.00 am and he had just taken delivery of a cup of his finest Kenyan roast from the receptionist, Samaira. The steaming cup sat on his expansive desk next to his briefcase. The events of the previous evening had annoyed him somewhat but he felt certain that after the pummelling he and Ali had given the young man, he would think twice before meddling in their affairs again. They had also given the white whore, Sharon, a few slaps as a warning that this should stop immediately. He sat there drinking coffee and idly browsing the internet while across the room the large flat screen television was tuned to the Sky News channel with the volume set on low. It was 5 minutes later that his attention was caught by a snippet of breaking news on the television. He lifted the remote control and quickly turned up the volume.

"Reports are coming in that there has been a large explosion on a residential street in the Finsbury Park area of North London. We will get more information to you just as soon as it comes in" said the concerned looking female news reader.

A frown formed on Akim Usmani's forehead and he sat forward to search on his computer for any updates. At that moment the screen on the television changed to a live view from a helicopter showing plumes of smoke rising from a strangely familiar residential street.

"La, bialtaakid la. hdha la ymkn 'an yakun.." he whispered as he stood up and walked towards the television 'No, surely not. This cannot be...'

As the view from the helicopter grew clearer he recognized the street as being his own but more importantly the flames and plumes of smoke were rising from his own house. The ticker tape that ran along the bottom the screen confirmed this and Akim Usmani stood there, completely gobsmacked and aghast as he watched the screen.

With his eyes still transfixed to the screen he pulled his phone from a pocket under his tunic and dialled the number for the land line at his house. The number immediately came back as unreachable. Next he tried the cell number of his wife but to no avail. It too came back as unreachable. Akim Usmani did not even have a number for his other son, Zain, so he called the number for Ali. Thankfully it rang and and Akim Usmani breathed a sigh of relief as it was answered immediately.

"Hello, Father.." came the cheerful, familiar voice.

"Alhamd lilah 'ajbat ya bunaya" he said quietly 'Thank God you answered, my son.'

"What's wrong father? You sound alarmed..."

"Where are you my son?"

"I'm at the takeaway, getting ready to open up. Why do you ask? What's wrong?"

"Turn on the news now!" said Akim "I will call you back shortly.."

Akim Usmani stood there and stared in horror at the screen. A crippling feeling of helplessness and indecision overcame him as the helicopter circled and focussed on the emergency services as they swarmed around on the street below. It was a full five minutes later when a semblance of sanity prevailed and he snapped out of the horror. *I must go there now.* He thought. Leaving his briefcase on his desk, he stormed out of his office and ran down the long corridor to the reception. The door burst open startling the receptionist, Samaira who was sitting at her computer behind her desk.

"I have to go now.." he mumbled as he made his way out into the cold.

Samaira stood up with a look of concern on her face and walked to the front doors of the warehouse showroom. She watched as her boss hurriedly climbed into his Volvo and sped off. Akim Usmani gripped the steering wheel and the tyres howled as he sped out of the gates to the Stone Industrial Estate. His mind was filled with a thousand thoughts and he found it hard to concentrate. He hooted at pedestrians and cyclists as he tore towards the bridge over the River Thames.

It was only when he got caught in a traffic jam near the river that his thoughts calmed down somewhat and he turned on the radio and tuned into the news. By then the news readers had identified the house number leaving him in no doubt at all that it was his house that had been destroyed. *But why? How did this happen?* He thought. *It can only be Zain. That filthy retarded imbecile must have something to do with it.* Suddenly the rushing wind of tinnitus returned in his ears but this time it was akin to a hurricane.

"Bastard!" he shouted, pounding at the steering wheel in frustration.

It was sitting there in the traffic jam that Akim Usmani slowly began putting together the pieces in his mind. Yes it was surely Zain who had caused this explosion but he also realized that due to this there would now be a very bright spotlight on him and his business activities. This was a cause for grave and immediate concern. Every part of his business and personal life would now be minutely scrutinized and exposed and this would surely result in his incarceration. There was a chance to avoid this but there were two very weak links in the chain. The white whore and whoever the young white man who had disturbed him the previous night. They both knew too much and if there ever was a hope for a return to some kind of normality they would both need to be out of the picture. *Yes.* He thought. *They have to go, and go now, before it's too late.* At this stage Akim Usmani had completely forgotten about the fate of his favourite son, Ali, and was solely focussed on his own survival. He needed to move and move fast. In the space of half an hour his world had changed forever and he needed to keep a cool head and think on his feet. It was twenty minutes later, as he was approaching Highbury, that Akim Usmani made a left turn and headed towards his secret safe house in Lower Holloway. He was going there to collect his gun.

CHAPTER THIRTY

Green

The massive explosion happened right in front of my eyes as if in slow motion. Its force was so great that I stumbled backwards and almost fell. It left my ears humming with a dull ache from the displaced air. Around me pieces of broken roof tiles and roof beams landed randomly with one denting the roof of the hire car.

"What the fuck?" I gasped wide eyed as I stared at the scene of destruction.

From what I could see there was little damage to the surrounding properties although most of their windows were blown in. The terrible weather had added to the fact that there had been few to no pedestrians on the quiet street and this was in fact a blessing. *You need to get out of here right now, Green. This was no accidental gas explosion.* With the cigarette still hanging from my lips I climbed into the vehicle, started it, and did a quick U-turn. A number of curious and panicked pedestrians were making their way down the street by the time I reached the junction and I could hear the sirens approaching in the distance. I crossed over the busy junction and made my way up the hill towards the Emirates Stadium and Highbury. As I drove I fought to gather my thoughts but the absolute and shocking suddenness of it still lingered and I battled to think straight. *There's only one thing that could have caused such a massive explosion, Green. The fucking Ammonium Nitrate in that fertilizer. There is no doubt about that. Your deepest fears have just been proven true. Just what are these people up to?* Eventually I passed the turn off to the stadium and reached the top of the hill. The BMW of Ali Usmani was still parked in the nearby alleyway and everything appeared to be normal. *It's like he doesn't even know. He can't do or he surely wouldn't be here still.* I shook my head and gunned the small engine in a rush to get back to my flat where I could sit down and attempt to put things into some kind of perspective. The rain continued falling and my mind was spinning as I took the fifteen minute drive back to my flat. I rushed upstairs without locking the door of the vehicle and immediately turned on the television news. As expected, the coverage was of the explosion I had just witnessed, with a helicopter now circling the site and a constant stream of video and verbal coverage. As I tried to get my thoughts in order it struck me that there was one missing person in all of this.

Akim Usmani. With the volume turned up loud on the television, I opened my laptop and clicked on the app for the tracking device I had placed in his briefcase. It took a minute to load up as usual and I drummed my fingers impatiently on the desk as I waited. *Where are you Usmani? Where are you right now?* Eventually the map on the screen opened and the blue dot showed. Akim Usmani was at his warehouse in the Stone Industrial Estate in South London. *These two fuckers are totally oblivious to this, Green. You know for sure there was someone in that upstairs room seconds before that thing went off. Zain more than likely. And what of the mysterious wife / mother? You also know that both Ali and his father were not there. They must be unaware of it!* My eyes flicked between the television and the tiny flashing blue dot on the laptop screen.

"What a total fucking mess..." I whispered to myself incredulously "A complete dog show."

At that moment my thoughts went back to Brandon. He had made no effort to call me and it was now almost 11.00 am. I stood up from my desk and walked over to the window to smoke as I called him. As before, the call rang until it went through to voicemail.

'Hi, you've reached Brandon Stevens. I'm not available to take your call right now but if you leave a message I'll get back to you as soon as I can.'

"Fuck!" I shouted out loud as I hung up and reached for the pack of cigarettes.

I tried calling him another seven times as I stood there smoking and staring out at the bleak grey landscape below, but each time to no avail. It was only then that a sneaking suspicion began crawling into the dark recesses of my mind. Until then, it would have been unthinkable but given the unbelievable events of the morning so far I found it difficult to put out of my mind. *What if the Usmani's have something to do with the fact that young Brandon isn't answering his phone? Given what's happened so far today, anything is possible, Green!*

"Nah..." I said quietly to myself as I crushed out the cigarette "Surely not. There must be a good reason for him not answering."

But the paranoid suspicion kept creeping back into my mind as I returned to sit at the desk to watch the television. *Focus. Focus, Green!* It was then that I had an idea. I picked up my phone and dialled the number for head office at the insurance firm. Eventually I got through to the human resources department and identified myself to the telephonist. It took some time to get the information I needed but eventually I was given a contact number and a land line for Brandon's mother's house in Wembley. Mrs Stevens answered almost immediately and I informed her who I was and asked if she knew where he was. The friendly sounding woman had a strong cockney accent similar to her son's.

"Ah hello Jason.." she said "Yes Brandon has told me all about you. He loves working with you I must say. Brandon left early this morning at around 6.00 am. He left me a note and I didn't even see him go.."

"Did you see him when he got home last night?" I asked calmly.

"Well, I didn't actually see him, but I spoke to him as he went to bed. He came home awfully late and I was in my own bed! Is there a problem, Jason?"

"Okay, I see.." I replied "No, no problem at all. Have a great day"

I hung up and once again walked to the window. *Well, at least you know he went home. But what about now? Where the hell is he?* I spent the next 20 minutes pacing the flat and racking my brain on what to do next. In the end I decided I had no choice. I had seen how upset the young man had been at the treatment of the girl. He had explained his attachment to her given her similarities to his own late sister. I felt certain he must have attempted to contact her again and this could be the only explanation as to his absence. *There's only one place he can be, Green.* With my mind made up, I wrapped up warmly in my jacket and scarf and headed out of the door and down to the hire car. My destination was Sharon Pennington's flat in the high rise blocks near Highbury.

CHAPTER THIRTY ONE

Akim Usmani

Akim Usmani parked his vehicle and ran through the rain towards his secret safe house in Lower Holloway. He quickly deactivated the alarm system and let himself in through the front door. Wasting no time, he took the stairs down to the basement area and unlocked the heavy steel door that separated the two spaces. Once inside he immediately began working the combination on the wall safe until the door swung open. Ignoring the piles of cash and the briquettes of heroin, he reached in and brought out the Czech CZ 75 pistol. The heavy feeling of it in his hands served to calm the constant rushing sound in his ears and brought on a strange feeling of serenity. *You need to think clearly.* He thought. He lifted his tunic, jammed the gun into his belt, and locked the safe once again. Leaving the steel partition door open, he dashed up the wooden stairs back to ground level. As he walked out of the house a plan was forming in his mind and he left the house without activating the alarm. The rain was still falling, albeit lighter, as he trotted down the street towards the parked Volvo station wagon. Akim Usmani's phone rang as he started the engine. It was from an unrecognised number and this sent a bolt of fear through his body. Tossing the phone on the passenger seat, he gunned the engine and sped off back towards Highbury. There was a build up of traffic as he approached the main road To Highbury and Akim Usmani was forced to slow down and go with the flow of it. All the while the radio constantly harped on about the explosion with more and more information coming through every minute. Again and again the phone rang and although he ignored it, it only served to accentuate his building rage and feelings of helplessness. Even the reassuring feeling of the gun in his belt could not calm the terrible raging winds in his ears. In a matter of hours his entire world had been turned upside down and would never be the same again. The fact that his wife and one son were very likely dead did not bother him in the slightest. His primary concern was for himself and Ali, and in that order. Eventually the traffic gave way and he was finally able to take the left turn to head up towards Highbury. It was 5 minutes later, as he was approaching Supreme Kebabs, that he saw the yellow checks and flashing blue lights of the police van. A number of officers were crowded around the entrance.

The sight of this sent a cold shiver down his spine as he realised that the whole house of cards was tumbling down rapidly. Although Akim Usmani loved his son, Ali, he realised that he was essentially weak. For years he had seen Ali as his only hope and had tried to instil strength and resolve in the boy, but deep down he knew that under interrogation the boy would crack and spill the beans on his entire operation. A great sadness filled his heart as he turned off the main road in an effort to avoid passing the shop. This sadness was soon replaced by a burning anger and a knowledge that unless he acted immediately, he would very likely be arrested and locked away for the rest of his life. The investigations would leave no stone unturned and every aspect of his personal and business life would be scrutinized minutely and exposed. Akim Usmani did a quick U-turn and headed back towards Highbury Park and the turn off that led down to the housing estate where Sharon Pennington lived. As he drove, his phone rang repeatedly and apart from glancing at the screen to see if there was a number he recognized, he ignored it. Akim Usmani's rage was so intense that his knuckles paled with the sheer force with which he gripped the steering wheel. His vision became tunnel like and even the voices on the radio and the sirens in the distance faded from his ears only to be replaced by the familiar and terrible rushing and howling wind. Despite the cold air coming in from the partially open driver's window, beads of sweat ran down his temples and into his thick beard. He made the left turn and drove down towards the grim and imposing set of 1970s tower blocks below. Akim Usmani parked his vehicle as near as he could to the courtyard between the towering behemoths. There was a lull in the rain and as he opened the driver's door he looked up towards the flat on the 17th floor of the building on the left where he knew the girl lived. *She knows too much and it seems he does too. She will be the magnet that draws the man from last night in. These two are the weak links in the chain and they need to be eliminated. The time is now!* Without locking the vehicle, he got out and casually walked into the giant concrete courtyard that lay between the group of towering buildings. The graffiti and litter that he would be normally be disgusted by did not bother him and eventually he crossed into the overhang at the entrance to the building.

There were a group of young children noisily kicking a football in the foyer but he ignored them and pushed the buttons on the lifts nearby. The lift on the right opened and he stepped inside and pushed the button for the 17th floor. The interior of the lift was clad with polished chrome and smelt of urine but even this did not bother him. He stood there patiently and felt the reassuring weight of the gun in his belt as he planned his next move. Eventually the doors opened and Akim Usmani stepped out and turned left and then right to head down the long walkway to the end flat where he knew the girl lived. On his left, all that separated him from the 54 metre drop to the concrete courtyard below was a low 4,5 ft wall with a thick steel bannister atop it. As he walked, he prepared himself mentally for what he might find when he knocked on the door. He was aware that the girl had come from a dysfunctional and alcoholic family so he expected little if any resistance. If there was, he would deal with it swiftly. Eventually he reached the door of the end flat and knocked on it four times. It took some time for it to be answered, but when it was, it was opened by a skinny middle aged woman in a faded tracksuit with bedraggled hair and hollow cheeks. A cigarette in need of ashing hung from her thin lips and she frowned and stared at him with confused, bloodshot eyes.

"Who are you?" she said in a husky voice.

"Good morning, I'm sorry to bother you but I am Sharon's boss Mr Usmani. Is she here by any chance?"

"Yeah..." slurred the clearly drunk woman "She's in her room with her new lad."

Akim Usmani smiled warmly at the woman. This unexpected news pleased him and would make the job a lot easier.

"Oh, that's great. I really need to speak to her. Would it be okay for me to pop in for a minute?"

The woman swayed on her feet and as she did, a length of ash fell from the cigarette between her lips.

"I ain't bothered.." she said with a shrug "She's in the room at the end of the hall."

Akim Usmani smiled graciously and bowed in gratitude.

"Thank you very much.." he said "I'll only be a minute."

The woman stood aside as Akim Usmani walked in. She smelt of alcohol and cigarettes but this did not bother him at all. The front room was cluttered and cloudy with stale smoke. At the far corner of the room on a couch sat a balding, overweight man in his forties. He wore nothing but a pair of underwear and a stained vest. Between his legs was a can of Carlsberg Special Brew extra strong lager. The man sat and stared at the blaring television screen opposite, completely paralytic and totally oblivious to his presence. Akim Usmani pulled the gun from his belt as he entered the corridor. The door at the far end was closed and he wasted no time reaching forward and opening it. The room was decorated in pink resembling a space that would normally be associated with a much younger girl. On the bed sat Sharon Pennington cross legged while the young man sat on wooden chair near a child's desk. Both of their faces registered abject shock and horror but they said nothing as he closed the door behind him. With the gun held out in front of him he spoke.

"Both of you, remain silent or I will kill you.." he said calmly.

The girl and the young man glanced at each other with wide eyes and then looked back at Usmani.

"You..." he said pointing the gun at Sharon "Get your jacket on. The three of us are going on a little trip together."

"But...." said the girl with a confused and terrified look on her face.

"Silence.." he hissed through gritted teeth, his dark eyes burning with rage.

Akim Usmani held the barrel of the gun to the temple of the terrified young man who sat on the chair nearby. Realizing this was no joke, the girl immediately stood up and began putting her puffy pink jacket on.

"Now.." said Usmani "You will both walk out of here calmly. I will be directly behind you and we will leave as if everything is completely normal. You will tell your mother there is something you need to attend to at work. One wrong move, and make no mistake, I will kill you. Do I make myself clear?"

"Yes.." came the solemn reply in unison.

Once the girl had zipped up her jacket, Akim Usmani motioned with the gun for Brandon to stand.

"Both of you" he said quietly "Stand by the door and get ready to leave."

With the three of them ready to move, Akim Usmani jammed the barrel of the pistol into the small of Brandon's back.

"Right.." he whispered "Open the door and walk out calmly. Remember, one wrong move and you're dead"

The group of three moved slowly down the corridor towards the smoke filled lounge. By the time they arrived in the main living room, Sharon's mother had taken her place on the couch next to the bald man. She too had opened a can of lager and was in the process of drinking it.

"Where are you going, Sharon?" she asked in slurred, husky voice.

"I have to go to work, Mum.." said the girl.

Without standing, the skinny woman shrugged with scornful disinterest and took another drink from the can.

"Suit yourself..." she mumbled in a cockney accent.

With Akim Usmani following closely behind, they turned left and walked towards the front door of the flat.

It was as Brandon was about to open the door that they heard someone knocking from the other side.

CHAPTER THIRTY TWO

Vertigo

My mind raced as I took the drive up to Highbury from my own area of Seven Sisters. The explosion had been a major news event and I knew its implications were more than serious. Added to that I still had the flash stick with my photographic and video evidence on the Usmani's. *It'll have to wait Green. Find Brandon first and then you can get on with that.* Eventually I arrived at the main road and headed left towards Highbury. It was 10 minutes later when I took the right turn that led down the cluster of tower blocks where Sharon Pennington lived. The rain fell lightly as I pulled into the car park near the central courtyard between the buildings. My mind was so preoccupied with the astonishing events of the morning that I failed to notice the Volvo station wagon parked nearby. Instead I parked as near as I could and looked up to the building on the left where I knew the girl lived. The wind had picked up and was blowing the light droplets of rain sideways. I climbed out of the vehicle, locked the door, and jogged across the bleak concrete courtyard through the rain until I reached the overhang at the entrance to the tower block. There were a group of young children kicking a football around in the foyer. Thankfully one of the lifts was on the ground floor and I quickly stepped in and pressed the button for the top floor. I stood there impatiently rocking on the balls of my feet as the lift ascended the 17 floors to the top. Eventually there was a dull electronic ping and the doors opened. A gust of freezing wind blew into the lift as I stepped out and turned left to reach the long walkway that led down the back of the building. I remembered clearly watching the girl entering the last flat on the top floor so I knew exactly where I was heading. As I took the walk I began preparing the afternoon. I would take Brandon to one side, explain the incredible events of the morning, and then we would both visit a nearby police station to make our reports. *Get that done and this whole shit show will be over, Green. And it couldn't come soon enough. You can finally wash your hands of it and be done with it. Let's just hope Brandon is here. He must be!* As usual, when it came to heights, I walked as far as I possibly could from the bannister. This fear of heights had been with me all my life and I had come to accept it would never be conquered. Instead I kept my vision directly ahead of me and avoided looking down at the 54 metre drop to my left.

My body was bitterly cold and my jacket soaked by the time I reached the end flat. I stood at the door and knocked on it three times. It came as something of a shock to see it open immediately and in front of me were the two faces of Brandon Stevens and Sharon Pennington. Initially there was a spilt second of relief in the knowledge that I had found him but this was very brief. It was only when I lifted my eyes did I see the dark, enraged face of Akim Usmani standing directly behind them.

"You!" he shouted as he lunged towards me pushing through Sharon and Brandon.

The whole thing happened in a spilt second and took me completely by surprise. Akim Usmani's huge hand hit me square in my chest and propelled me backwards towards the low wall and bannister behind me. Such was the suddenness and sheer force of the blow, I had absolutely no time to prepare for it. I hit the bannister with small of my back and my legs came up and over in a wild and uncontrolled tumble. In the back of my mind I heard the girl scream but this was soon dulled by the expectation of the fall and my own imminent death. Suddenly everything was in slow motion as I watched my own legs above me silhouetted against the dreary grey sky above. In that instant there was brief moment of serenity and clarity of thought in my mind. *Well, this is unexpected, Green. Never thought you'd go this way did you? Had to happen some time I guess.* But by some stroke of luck or perhaps a primitive instinct for survival, my right hand gripped the tubular cold wet steel of the bannister as my body tumbled over the wall. The full weight of my tumbling body twisted my arm and I slammed head and front first into the wet concrete of the outer wall. I felt my arm would be ripped from the shoulder socket and I hung there winded and disorientated for the next 10 seconds as I gasped for air. In the back of my mind I waited for the blow to my right hand that would dislodge it from the cold steel of the bannister and send me tumbling to my death below. But it never came. Instead I hung there gasping and wheezing as I tried to get oxygen back into my lungs. Eventually I opened my eyes only to see the terrifying 54 metre drop below me. Instantly my legs began to tingle uncontrollably as the ghastly spinning sensation of vertigo overwhelmed me. This frozen terror was only broken by the sensation of losing my grip on the bannister and the excruciating aching of my arm and shoulder.

I reached up with my left hand and gripped the bannister as hard as I could. I hung there like a bat with my eyes screwed shut as I fought to control the vertigo. *Don't look down, whatever you do. Don't look down.* Once again, in the back of my mind I wondered when the blows would come to my hands. I had been expecting them for some time. Still there was nothing. A minute later and I had gathered the strength to pull myself up and hook my right leg over the concrete wall below the steel bannister. Using the strength of my left arm I pulled myself up further until eventually I tumbled over the bannister and fell to safety onto the hard, wet surface of the walkway. I opened my eyes to see a confused looking and clearly drunk woman staring down at me. She swayed on her feet as she hung onto the open door of the flat. Still panting heavily from the exertion, I slowly sat up clutching my right shoulder.

"What's going on here?" asked the woman in a husky voice.

Ignoring her, I slowly got to my feet. It was clear Usmani had left the scene immediately after pushing me from the balcony. Perhaps he had no idea I had been able to hang on. Gripping the bannister with my left hand, I looked down to the courtyard below. It was then I saw the three of them. Usmani, Brandon and Sharon were approaching the parked Volvo station wagon. Even from that height I could see the pistol in his hand. It was plainly obvious they were being taken against their will and I watched as Brandon climbed into the driver's seat of the vehicle with Sharon to his left in the passenger seat. Before climbing into the back seat of the vehicle, Akim Usmani paused briefly and looked up to where I stood on the 17th floor of the building. Even from that height our eyes met briefly, and I whispered a silent promise.

"Be sure of this" I said quietly "I *am* going to kill you.."

CHAPTER THIRTY THREE

Usmani

"Walk faster!" hissed Akim Usmani through gritted teeth as he hurried Brandon and Sharon across the courtyard.

The barrel of the pistol was still held to the small of Brandon's back under his jacket. The terrified couple complied and picked up their pace as the freezing drizzle fell about them. Akim Usmani glanced around the courtyard for the body of the man he had pushed from the balcony. It was a face he remembered as the man who had visited his warehouse the previous day. A man by the name of Green. There was nothing. *No body. The man must have clung on somehow?* But his sense of urgency and the need to get away was such that he saw no point in wasting any more time. A minute later the three of them arrived at the parked Volvo station wagon.

"You!" he said to Brandon, pressing the barrel harder into his back "Get in the driver's seat and Sharon, you get in next to him in the passenger seat."

Brandon and Sharon complied and as they did Akim Usmani readied himself to climb in the back seat behind Brandon. Before he did so he glanced once more at the courtyard and then up to 17th floor of the building. Standing there, clutching the balcony, was the man he had just tried to throw off. Even from that height, their eyes met and Akim Usmani scowled with anger before climbing into the vehicle.

"Start the engine!" he barked in Brandon's ear as he handed him the keys. "Drive!"

Brandon reversed the Volvo and made a left out of the parking lot. At that moment, Sharon Pennington began to whimper and cry softly.

"Silence, you filthy whore!" shouted Usmani as he held the barrel of the gun to the back of her head.

Brandon drove slowly up the hill towards the main road. As he did so his phone rang in his pocket.

"Hand me your phone!" said Usmani "You too, Sharon!"

The pair complied immediately and Akim Usmani opened the window of the vehicle and threw both phones violently down onto the tarmac where they smashed into little pieces.

"Turn left here..." he said as they reached the main road at the top of the hill opposite Highbury Park.

The next five minutes were spent in stony silence as the Volvo made its way through the drizzle and the heavy afternoon traffic. Eventually they reached the turn off to Lower Holloway.

"Make a right here" said Usmani "Slow and steady.."

Brandon Stevens glanced at the man sitting behind him in the rear view mirror. He appeared to have calmed down somewhat. But in reality, Akim Usmani's mind was in turmoil and beads of sweat ran down his temples into his thick beard. He shifted in his seat and his eyes darted from side to side constantly. The terrible rushing sound of wind in his ears came in random waves and they were all encompassing. It was 10 minutes later that they arrived at the quiet street where Akim Usmnai's secret safe house was located.

"Park here.." he said as he looked around.

The weather had ensured there was little or no pedestrian traffic on the street and all around was quiet.

"Right.." said Usmani "You are both going to get out of the vehicle and walk calmly up the street in front of me. Remember, one wrong move and I will kill you. Do you understand?"

"Yes..." came the solemn reply in unison from the front of the vehicle.

"Let's go, now.."

With Brandon and Sharon walking in front as instructed, the three made their way through the rain to the plain looking semi detached house up the street. As they reached the front door, Usmani reached forward to hand Brandon the keys. Once inside, he closed the door behind him and with the gun still in hand, he spoke.

"There is a small wooden door under the stairwell" he said. "Sharon, you walk in front, open it and we will follow you downstairs."

The three of them made their way down the narrow staircase to the cold, darkened space below. Akim Usmani flicked a switch on the wall which illuminated the area. The thick concrete wall with the open steel door stood directly in front of them. Beyond that lay the sparsely furnished room with the banknote counter and the wall safe.

"Carry on.." said Usmani "Into that room."

Brandon and Sharon walked into the bright, empty space and stood waiting for the next instruction.

"Sit down against the wall over there.." said Usmani pointing to his left with the pistol "And don't move."

Brandon and Sharon did exactly as instructed. The concrete floor was cold and they watched as Akim Usmani walked over to the large wall safe at the far side of the room. The room was silent apart from the soft clicking of the combination lock of the safe as he spun it to open it. As he did so he glanced repeatedly over his shoulder, gun still in hand, to ensure they had not moved. Eventually the heavy door of the safe swung open and Akim Usmani reached into the interior of the safe. The bundles of hard cash he removed totalled over £65000.00 and he placed the money on the plain pine table near the banknote counter. He retrieved a black plastic bag from the bottom of the safe and proceeded to stuff the bundles of banknotes in it.

Once done, he closed the safe and spun the combination wheel to ensure it was locked. Finally he turned and picked up the bag with his left hand. He stood there as if in deep thought as he regarded Brandon and Sharon sitting on the concrete floor. The moment only lasted seconds then Akim Usmani walked swiftly towards the steel door at the back of the room. Once out, he slammed the door closed noisily and slid the two heavy dead bolts shut. Leaving the interior lights on, he fixed and locked the two padlocks on the dead bolts, effectively trapping Brandon and Sharon in the safe room. Wasting no time, he raced up the narrow wooden stairway and left the house after activating the alarm system. Akim Usmani walked through the rain until he reached his vehicle. He climbed into the driver's seat, closed the door, and sat there deep in thought. Through the rushing winds of rage he heard in his ears there was a new emotion coming through. Fear. He knew he had to flee, and do so immediately, but there was one thing he had forgotten. In his rush to leave the warehouse he had neglected to pick up his briefcase. Akim Usmani glanced at his watch then looked around the quiet street. He took a deep breath, pushed the key into the ignition, started the engine and drove off into the gloomy afternoon.

CHAPTER THIRTY FOUR

Green

I stood there panting heavily and turned to look at the woman swaying in the doorway. It was clear she was beyond drunk and I realised then that she would be of no use to me at all. Looking back down towards the road I saw the Volvo station wagon heading up the hill towards Highbury. My shoulder was aching deeply and I stood there rubbing it gently with my left hand as I struggled to think of my next move. *The tracking device, Green. You need to track that bastard now!* With the woman still standing in the doorway, I turned and took the walk back to the lifts at the far side of the building. The children who had been playing with the football in the foyer were totally oblivious to what had just happened as I walked out of the building and ran through the rain across the courtyard to my vehicle. I was consumed with fear for the safety of Brandon and the girl as I took the short drive home through the afternoon traffic. *Where might Usmani have taken them?* I knew full well that he was more than capable of harming them. Possibly worse. Realising I was frozen cold and probably in a state of shock, I made my way upstairs and changed my wet clothes immediately. I took a couple of pain killers for my shoulder and boiled the kettle for coffee as I waited for my laptop to boot up. I opted for my original blend of brew having decided that I no longer liked the taste of Kenyan coffee. It had left a particularly bitter taste in my mouth. I tried three times to call Brandon but every time it simply went through to voice mail. Finally I sat at my desk and opened the website for the tracking device in Usmani's briefcase. As usual, it took a while to load but when it did it showed that the device was still in the industrial estate in South London. I did a quick check on its travel history for the day and it showed it had been stationary since morning. I sat back in my chair to think. *What the hell is going on here? He's never without that briefcase. It's always with him.* I stood up and took the steaming mug of coffee over to the window to smoke. *There are only two possible scenarios here, Green. Either he has found the device and dumped it, or he simply left his briefcase at the warehouse. Perhaps he did this by accident when he heard about the explosion. Yes, that must be the reason.* As I stood there I tried to put myself in Akim Usmani's position. *If it was you, what would you do? Where would you go?*

I ended up pacing the room for the next five minutes. Things were moving so swiftly I had difficulty ordering my own thoughts. Eventually I decided there were only two courses of action. Firstly, I needed to deliver the flash stick with the photo and video evidence to the police, and secondly, I needed to get to where that tracking device was. *He will return to his briefcase, Green. And that tracking device will lead you to him and ultimately to Brandon and Sharon. You need to move, and move fast!* With my mind made up, I walked back to my laptop and began typing an anonymous letter to the police. There was no time to sit making a lengthy report in what would no doubt be a very busy station. *No, you need to drop off the letter and get moving immediately*. The letter was short and to the point. It explained the pictures and videos on the flash stick and gave the address and names of the owners of the flat. I knew it wouldn't be long before they made the link with the explosion but I had no time to waste. Once done, I printed the letter and placed it along with the flash stick in an envelope on which I wrote 'The Officer In Charge. Urgent'. Finally I sat back and racked my brain for anything else that needed doing. I could think of nothing so I wrapped up warmly and headed out taking the envelope and my laptop with me. The drive to the police station at Highbury took only 10 minutes and I parked the vehicle around the back of the station leaving the laptop under the seat. The rain held off as I took the walk around the building and in through the front entrance. As expected, there was a fair amount of activity given there had just been a massive explosion in the next borough. I approached the female officer on duty at the front desk and calmly handed her the envelope.

"What's this?" she asked curiously.

"I'm not sure.." I said "My boss asked me to drop it off."

The officer shrugged nonchalantly and I turned to leave. I felt her eyes on me as I walked out of the building.

Perhaps she saw the strain on your face, Green? God knows it's been a hell of a day so far. I left the building without event and made my way back around to the parked vehicle.

Once inside I started the engine to warm the interior and retrieved the laptop from under the seat. It only took a minute to plug my phone into the USB port for mobile internet and I sat there drumming my fingers on the steering wheel as I waited for the tracking site to boot up. When, finally it did, I was surprised to see that Usmani was on the move. In one way it came as a relief that he had not found the device and I would be able to follow and find him. But then there was the worry and fear for the safety of Brandon and the girl. The vehicle was heading South towards the M25 motorway. *Where are you going Usmani? Where are you taking them?* I tried to call Brandon's phone once again, but like before, it went straight to voicemail. I placed the open laptop on the passenger seat, plugged it in using an adaptor to the cigarette lighter, and started the engine. It was time to find Mr Akim Usmani.

CHAPTER THIRTY FIVE

Usmani

It took forty minutes in the afternoon traffic for Akim Usmani to reach his warehouse in the Stone Industrial Estate in South London. During the drive his emotions had swung between seething rage and cold fear. The fear was that the police would be there already and he would be unable to make good his escape. During the drive his phone had rung repeatedly and this had further added to his fury. Eventually he pulled into the estate in the gloomy afternoon light and cautiously approached his warehouse. From a distance he could see no activity that was out of the usual. He drove round the block twice to make sure there was nothing untoward going on before pulling up to his usual parking place at the front of the building. Reaching down to his left, he placed the black plastic bag of cash under the passenger seat then climbed out of the car and locked it. The freezing drizzle had started falling again as he made his way up the concrete walkway to the front entrance of Akus Trading. Ignoring the startled looking Samaira, he quickly made his way to the warehouse access door and down the long corridor to his office. Once inside he grabbed his briefcase and quickly rummaged through it to check his passport was there. Akim Usmani breathed a sigh of relief when he saw the passport was still there in one of the rear compartments.

"Alshukr Lilah" he whispered to himself. 'Thank God.'

Akim Usmani closed the briefcase and held it by the handle in his right hand. He paused to look through the window behind his desk into the cavernous warehouse beyond. The pallets and stacks of tiles and coffee represented his life's work. Decades of his own hard toil and dedication had been destroyed in an instant. Suddenly the terrible howling wind in his ears returned. His eyes darkened and his knuckles paled with the sheer force with which he gripped the briefcase. *Calm down. Calm down.* His tunic billowed as he spun around and walked out of his office and back up the corridor towards the reception.

Ignoring the receptionist once again, he rushed through the front of the building and out into the damp, rapidly darkening afternoon. With a cursory glance around the area, he quickly climbed into the Volvo and closed the door. Wasing no time, he reached under the passenger seat and retrieved the plastic bag of cash which he emptied and placed in the briefcase. Finally he glanced nervously in the rear view mirror as he turned the ignition key. The estate and surrounds were all quiet and appeared normal to him as he pulled away and drove back towards the gates to the complex. Akim Usmani made a left and headed South towards the busy M25 motorway that is the ring road for the greater London area. It was 10 minutes later when he pulled off to the side and parked near near a tatty looking convenience store somewhere in the bleak and depressing urban sprawl of South London. His hands shook slightly as he picked up his phone and began to search for last minute flights out of the UK from Heathrow Airport. It was as he was browsing his options that the phone rang, once again it was from an unrecognised number. For him, this was the last straw and the howl of a rapidly building hurricane raged in his ears. The veins in his neck bulged and Akim Usmani held his head back and let out a deep, inhuman scream similar to that of a wounded buffalo. A group of teenagers nearby saw this spectacle and quickly hurried away in the opposite direction. With tears of white hot fury, he looked down at the ringing phone. At that moment he felt his head might explode with the pressure and he had to physically fight the overwhelming urge to crush the device in his hands. It was some minutes later when he had calmed down sufficiently to carry on browsing the many flights on the website. Eventually he found one and booked and paid for it immediately. The flight was due to leave from Heathrow Terminal 4 at 7.00 pm that very evening. Akim Usmani glanced at his watch. The time had just gone 3.30 pm. *I'll make it*. He thought. *Plenty of time*. The rain was falling once again as he pulled off on his way to the M25 motorway and Heathrow Airport. Once again his knuckles were white as he gripped the steering wheel and fought the urge to plough into the innocent pedestrians that crossed the road ahead.

CHAPTER THIRTY SIX

Green

"No, no, no, fuck!" I shouted as I saw the long line of backed up traffic heading down towards the Islington Angel.

I turned to take a look at the screen of the laptop that sat on the passenger seat next to me and saw that the Volvo was about to filter onto the M25 motorway. I knew full well that it would pick up speed from there on and could head off in any direction. Realising there was absolutely nothing I could do about it I reached into my pocket and pulled out the packet of cigarettes. As I smoked my mind constantly went back to the vision of Akim Usmani forcing Brandon and the girl into the vehicle. *Where is he taking them? Has he harmed them?* I shifted constantly in my seat and glanced at the laptop screen repeatedly as the traffic edged forward at a snail's pace through the city.

It was some 30 infuriating minutes later, as I was crossing the Thames, that I saw the tracking device had finally come to a halt at Heathrow airport. *What the hell?* I drummed my fingers on the steering wheel as I thought about this unexpected turn of events. *Either he is dumping the vehicle there and this is a ruse, or he is actually going somewhere. But if he is going somewhere, where are Brandon and Sharon?* These never ending questions and worries stayed with me until I reached the M25 motorway 20 minutes later and was finally able to accelerate. By then the sky was darkening rapidly and I cursed under my breath as I realised I had wasted most of the afternoon. By then the tracker was showing it had entered the actual building of Heathrow Terminal 4. Knowing it was only 30 miles from where I was, I crossed into the inside lane and put my foot down. Ultimately this proved futile as soon after the traffic became backed up once again and one of the overhead illuminated signs indicated there had been an accident at a nearby junction and to expect delays.

"Fuck!" I shouted as I pounded the steering wheel.

By then my nerves were frayed, my shoulder was aching, and I was feeling totally exhausted.

The long queue of backed up vehicles inched forward until we had passed the scene of the accident. It turned out it was minor incident at a nearby off ramp but it had been enough for the police to close off one of the lanes. I floored the accelerator and sped off towards Heathrow Terminal 4 weaving dangerously in between the cars and trucks that filled the four lanes. I arrived at the airport at 5.40 pm and immediately drove to the short stay car park. I carried the laptop with me on the short walk to the main terminal building and spent the next 10 minutes walking around the front area desperately searching for Usmani. With the search proving fruitless I made my way to the nearest coffee shop and sat down to get online. The blue dot showed that the tracking device was in the same building not more than 100 metres from where I sat. Akim Usmani had made it through check in and security and was about to board a plane to a destination unknown and I had obviously just missed him. *Fuck!* I looked around the busy terminal and saw an information desk not far from where I sat. I closed the laptop and walked over to make some enquiries. The lady behind the desk, although friendly and helpful, was unable to give me any information as to where Akim Usmani was headed. She explained that it a security matter and this was information she was simply not allowed to give out. She could not even confirm that he had checked in. I thanked her and turned to walk towards the departure gates. I stopped 30 metres away and paused to think. I had to fight an overwhelming urge to sprint through the gates and barge my way into the departure lounge. It was clear I was faced with an extremely important decision. *Akim Usmani is alone. That much is indisputable. That means he must have left Brandon and Sharon somewhere in the greater London area. Pray they're alive, Green. The man is a monster. Pure evil. And he is more than capable of killing them. Think, and think fast!* I looked behind me and saw a billboard for the Hilton Hotel Heathrow. The sign boasted it was within walking distance under a covered walkway. I stared at it as my mind went through the various courses of action available to me. It was 10 minutes later when I arrived at the reception of the hotel. When asked how long I would be staying I could give no clear answer so I booked and paid for one night. The room would allow me to rest and prepare, and would also have full internet service for me to track Usmani. I knew full well that the tracking device would not work in a commercial aircraft unless held up to a window. There was simply too much steel surrounding it from the body of the plane.

I knew I would have to wait until he reached his destination wherever that may be. As I stood in the lift heading up to my room on the 8th floor I realized I wasn't carrying my passport. *Shit!* I pulled my phone from pocket and called the only other person who had keys for my flat. My cleaner was an elderly lady from Poland who had worked for me three times weekly for the past 5 years. Often in the past she had made sure my flat was cleaned when I had been out of the country on work or on holiday. I was fond of her and trusted her implicitly. She answered the phone immediately and agreed to go to the flat, open up, pack a small bag of clothes and my passport and deliver it to the hotel. I told her to also pack the small black bag of surveillance equipment that I kept at the top of my cupboard as well. I promised to pay her a week's wages for the trouble for which she was more than delighted. Living in the nearby suburb of Manor House would mean that it would be an easy trip for her to my flat and a simple, straightforward journey on the tube to Heathrow. She told me she would make sure my bag was with me within 2 hours to which I thanked her and hung up. The room was spacious and comfortable with views over the airport and runways. I stood at the window and looked out at the silent twinkling lights of the airport and surrounds. The sky was jet black and droplets of rain ran down the glass. Feeling tired, I made a cup of coffee, plugged in the laptop, and lay down on the bed. With the television news on and the computer nearby I watched the blue dot on the screen and drank coffee in an effort to stay awake. It was at exactly 6.30 that the blue dot began to move. I sat up to watch it as it did. It was not long after that it suddenly disappeared from the screen. *He's in the aeroplane now, Green. No doubt about it.* I knew that for the device to work properly, it needed to have uninterrupted access to at least 4 satellites. That was the nature of GPS. In the body of a commercial airliner this was impossible and it would remain that way for the duration of the flight. *Nothing for it, Green. You'll have to wait until it pings again. Wherever that may be.*

My bag and passport were delivered at 7.25 pm and I gratefully paid for the favour in cash. As promised, the black bag of surveillance equipment was there along with a good selection of clothing. Finally I lay back on the bed once again with a stream of rolling thoughts spinning through my mind.

My body ached and I was shattered tired from the worry and the frantic events of the day. In my mind I kept reliving the images of Akim Usmani in the flat with the unfortunate drug dealer who had lost his thumb nail. The sheer speed and explosive violence of it all was a grim reminder that the fact that Brandon and Sharon Pennington were missing did not bode well. It was not long after that I felt my eyelids begin to close. I fought it for another few minutes but drifted off into a deep dreamless sleep. I awoke with a start exactly 7 hours later. At first I was confused as to where I was but then it all came back to me. I sat up suddenly and felt the deep ache in my torn shoulder as I rubbed my eyes and stood up to go and wash my face. The time was 3.00 am and I hurried back to the laptop cursing quietly at having overslept. There was still no tiny flashing blue light and the screen showed the same picture it had done when the tracker had stopped transmitting. After trying Brandon's phone once again to no avail I boiled the kettle and made a cup of coffee which I carried down the corridor to the fire escape. The rain had stopped but the wind howled around the building chilling me to my bones as I smoked. The fact that I was five floors up brought back memories of the terrible vertigo and terror I had suffered when Usmani had tried to throw me from the building in Highbury. I flicked the cigarette butt into the darkness and quickly made my way back to the warmth of my room. I sat in front of the screen mentally willing the tiny flashing blue dot to return. In the back of my mind I began to fear that it had stopped working for some reason. Perhaps the battery had failed and it had been rendered useless? *No, Green. That device cost well over £2000 and is of the highest quality. It is commonly used by intelligence agencies the world over. Hold firm. It'll show up.* It was half an hour and another cup of coffee later when I heard the ping from the laptop. I had been standing at the window fretting about Brandon and the girl when I heard it. I spun around, spilling some coffee on the carpet in the process as I walked to the desk. I sat in front of the screen to see the previous map was gone and the image was pixelated as the GPS triangulated itself to pinpoint its new location.

"Come on, come on.." I said with gritted teeth as I waited.

Suddenly the screen cleared and in the centre the familiar blue dot flashed. I frowned as I read the name of the location in the bottom left corner of the screen.

"Jomo Kenyatta International Airport.." I said under my breath "Kenya. The fucker has fled to Kenya!"

I sat there flabbergasted as I stared at the screen. Then it all started to make sense. *The man has a business there, Green. The coffee factory. It makes sense he would flee there. He's probably got assets there as well as money. Plus it's a good place to disappear. Africa always is. But what about Brandon and the girl? Are they dead or alive? What the fuck are you gonna do now, Green?* Desperate for a cigarette, I left the room once again and walked down the corridor to the fire exit. The night was pitch black and there was no change in the weather but my mind was too occupied to worry about the cold. As I smoked I watched the flashing lights of a plane as it came in to land on the nearby runway. *What's the answer, Green? You know the answer. Time is the most important thing here, and it's running out fast. You need to go and find this man now. Brandon and Sharon are either dead or they are being held somewhere. You need to go to him now!* It took me less than 10 minutes to book the trip. There was a Qatar Airways flight to Nairobi leaving from Terminal 4 at 7.00 am that morning with a short stop in Doha. Thankfully it was an ongoing flight and would only be stopping to pick up passengers en route to Kenya. I would arrive in Nairobi at 4.00 pm in the afternoon and immediately proceed to wherever the tracking device led me. It took less than 10 minutes to book a vehicle from Avis Rent-A-Car online. The Ford Ranger pickup I booked was fully kitted out for off road travel should it be necessary and it was also fitted with satellite navigation. The combination of that plus the tracking device would ensure I would be able to locate Usmani anywhere. With everything in place I sat back and clicked on the page for the tracking device. By then it had moved from the main airport building and was moving in the streets of Nairobi. I had never been to Kenya although I knew that its capital was a huge bustling city with over 5 million inhabitants. Finally I stood up and headed for a long shower. I felt grimy and my nerves were frayed from the tension and worry. I stood under the powerful jets of hot water with my eyes closed as I ran through the astonishing events of the past few days. What had started out as a simple plug and play insurance fraud case had degenerated into something far darker and deadly. Lives had been lost and more were at stake and I was under no illusion as to the dangers I would be facing.

The man had tried to kill me once already and his recent temperament and behaviour was similar to that of a caged and cornered wild animal. There was no time to waste after my shower so I packed my bag and headed down to the reception to check out. I made one final call to Brandon's phone but as before, it went straight to voicemail.

The security and check in process in the airport terminal took forty minutes and finally I walked into the departure area feeling unsure of what to expect. One thing I knew for sure was I had to get to Usmani as soon as possible. One way or another I would find out what had become of Brandon Stevens and Sharon Pennington. I wasted no time in getting to the departure gate and sat drinking coffee until the flight was called at 6.20 am. The Qatar Airways Airbus A330 was spacious and I took my window seat in economy class and waited for the push back and taxi. It was still totally dark when the giant jet accelerated and took off and I watched the twinkling lights of London gradually fade below as the aircraft gained altitude. I put my seat back and closed my eyes to try to get some sleep but my brain was wired from the coffee and the expectation of what was to come. Ahead of me lay the unknown and I knew it would not be easy. But if there was one place on earth I knew best, it was my destination, Africa.

CHAPTER THIRTY SEVEN

Usmani

Akim Usmani's forehead was furrowed by deep lines of stress and worry. His dark eyes were bloodshot and the skin surrounding them was smudged a dark bluish colour from fatigue. Carrying only his briefcase, he strode through the arrivals door and into the main airport concourse. He paused briefly to look at the sleepy looking crowd of onlookers awaiting the passengers from the early morning flight. The time was 4.00 am and although the temperature in Jomo Kenyatta International Airport was a pleasant 17 degrees Celsius, dark patches of sweat showed from under the armpits of of his dark grey tunic. Awaiting his arrival at the back of a crowd was a tall Kenyan man by the name of Elijah Mwangi. At 44 years old, he had been working for Akus Trading for the past 10 years and had slowly risen through the ranks to his current position of general manager. A proud son of Kikuyu parents, he stood at over 6 foot tall and his elevated position in the company had resulted in him being particularly fond of the finer things in life like drink, women, and takeaway food. As a result Elijah Mwangi was grossly overweight and he wiped the sweat from his cannonball like bald head with a damp handkerchief as he waited for his boss. It had been another night of heavy drinking at the nearby shebeen in

Naru village and the unexpected call to drive to Nairobi to collect his boss had come as something of a shock. Upon seeing his boss, he barged through the crowd and walked up to him with a broad but nervous smile.

"Good morning, sir.." he said in his deep voice "Welcome back to Kenya."

Elijah Mwangi bowed slightly but kept his hands at his sides. He knew full well that his boss would never stoop so low as to shake hands with a black employee.

"Where is your luggage sir?" he asked with a puzzled look on his rotund face.

"I have no luggage!" snapped Usmani "Now, let us go to Kutus immediately!"

The two big men walked out of the arrivals hall and into the steamy humidity of the predawn Kenyan morning. The air was tinged with the smell of aviation fuel as they crossed the road and made their way into the multi storey car park on the other side.

One of the perks of his position as general manager of the coffee packing firm was the use of company vehicles. The Toyota Land Cruiser was almost 10 years old but was powerful, reliable, and handled the rough roads of Kirinyaga County with ease. Elijah Mwangi had made sure the vehicle had been meticulously cleaned when he received the call announcing the imminent arrival of his boss. The alarm beeped once as the two men approached and the central locking mechanism disengaged. Akim Usmani climbed into the passenger seat and placed the briefcase in the foot well while Elijah took his place behind the wheel. The first thing he became aware of when he closed the door was the smell of body odour. Suddenly a rush of wind sounded in his ears and his hands closed into fists as he closed his eyes to ride it out. Elijah turned to smile at his boss as he started the vehicle but quickly looked away sensing all was not well. He was fully aware of the man's fiery temperament. The drive out of the airport grounds took only a few minutes and Elijah made a right turn heading North towards the A2 highway which is the main route to the town of Thika. Akim Usmani was relieved he would not have to endure the mind numbing traffic of the Nairobi city centre which was known to back up sometimes before sunrise. It was still dark when Elijah made a right at the turn off near the Karura forest and headed North East up the A2 road. It was only then that Akim Usmani felt he could breathe once again. He had escaped the inevitable in London and now he would be free to rebuild his life. Perhaps one day he would return to the UK but for now at least he was safe. Soon enough they left the Nairobi area and headed out into the darkness towards Kiambu County and the industrial town of Thika. The sun began to rise as the vehicle approached the busy town and already street traders and hawkers were gathering on the roadside pushing carts of goods and congregating at bus stops. The roads in the small city were potholed and littered and already the traffic had started throwing up dust and causing delays. Akim Usmani sat in angry silence as their progress was slowed until eventually he snapped.

"Just put your foot down, will you?" he said bitterly "Get out of this shit hole."

Elijah turned nervously to look at his boss.

"Yes sir.." he said.

Eventually they left the confines of the city and drove out onto the open veld once again. The African dawn cast a bright pink hue across the horizon and in the distance the mountains of Kirinyaga County came into view. The open road allowed Elijah to speed up and within 40 minutes they had reached them. As they gained altitude the foliage around them began to change from dry African savannah to lush green Afro montane forest. The soil changed colour to the nutrient rich red earth of coffee growing country. Thick green vines and massive strangler figs hung from the trees as the road began to wind its way up into the hills. The air began to cool noticeably and Akim Usmani breathed a sigh of relief. It was 6.45 am when they finally arrived at the quaint mountain town of Kutus. Surrounded on all sides by green mountains, the main industry there was agriculture. Although slightly ramshackle, the streets were ordered and less littered than other towns in Kenya. The locals were known for being of a pleasant disposition and there was a friendly small town feel to the place. Elijah drove into the city centre and took a left on the main street near the old colonial railway station. Soon enough the tarred road ended and they began the steep climb on a rough dirt road to the nearby village of Naru where the Akus Trading coffee packing factory was located. Recent heavy rains had resulted in the road being somewhat slippery but there was no need to engage four wheel drive. Ten minutes later they arrived at the small mountain village of Naru with its single street lined with bars and general dealers. Akim Usmani sat forward in his seat and glanced up the hill towards the walled and gated compound that was Akus Trading. Surrounded on three sides by steep hills and thick green jungle, the 2 acre site consisted of a bean drying yard, a packing warehouse, with a double storey building at the rear that would be his home for the foreseeable future. Elijah pulled up to the sliding gate and hooted. Immediately the gate slid open pushed by a skinny young man dressed in dark blue overalls. The guard saluted the occupants of the vehicle with a flourish as it drove through into the drying yard. Even at that early hour, a group of around 30 women were busy spreading raw coffee beans on the long rows of wide tables lined in front of the packing warehouse. The beans would remain there drying in the sun until evening when they would be repacked into their large hessian sacks and stored in the warehouse. The women turned to look at the vehicle as it passed them but Akim Usmani sat staring forward and ignored them completely.

They drove up the hill to the double storey building at the back of the property where Elijah parked in a car port to the left.

"Now, sir.." he said nervously "We have arrived."

Akim Usmani grunted and stepped out of the vehicle carrying his briefcase. His muscles were stiff and his bones ached as he slammed the door of the vehicle and turned to look at the view. Below him lay the sprawling 2 acre compound with its tall concrete wall around the perimeter. Further down, in the valley below, the town of Kutus lay nestled in the wide valley of the surrounding green mountains. The air was crisp and cool and morning was quiet.

"Open the house, Elijah" said Usmani who stood nearby waiting.

The building was in need of maintenance with patches of peeling paint and one smashed window pane on the upper floor. It had been 2 years since Usmani had last visited. Elijah walked quickly to the arch topped front door which was fashioned from dark teak railway sleepers. It took some time to open the door as the lock had stuck from being neglected for so long. Eventually the two men walked into the hallway at the front of the house and then further into the lounge area. Although the inside was clean, the air was stale and musty and it was clear no one had set foot in the place for a long time.

"What sort of manager are you?" said Usmani quietly as he looked around "You haven't even opened the windows to air the place out."

Elijah Mwangi dropped his gaze to floor in shame.

"Sorry sir.." he mumbled forlornly "Your arrival was very sudden."

Akim Usmani turned and looked at the view below through the dusty windows. He felt dehydrated from the flight and unwashed. He had been wearing the same clothes since the morning of the previous day.

"You may go now, Elijah" he said "Leave the vehicle. I will be going shopping later. From now you will be using the Mazda pickup for your transport.

"Yes sir.." said Elijah with a bow.

Akim Usmani watched as his manager turned and made his way to the door.

"One more thing Elijah" he said "If anyone comes here asking questions about me. Anyone at all. You let me know immediately, is that clear?"

Elijah nodded in understanding.

"I will be here for a while" said Usmani "Anyone asking questions about me or my whereabouts, you let me know. Do this right and there will be a brand new company vehicle for you. Understood?"

"Yes sir..." said Elijah, his eyes lighting up at the thought "Of course, I will do so..."

"Good" replied Usmani "You may leave now."

Elijah Mwangi turned and made his way to the door. He closed it behind him and began walking down to the packing warehouse below.

CHAPTER THIRTY EIGHT

Green

"Welcome to Nairobi sir" said the young man at the car hire desk "Business or pleasure?"

"Business.." I replied "And I'm running late. If we could get this done as quickly as possible that would be great."

"Certainly sir" he replied sensing my urgency.

I had sat awake fretting over Brandon and Sharon until we had landed in Doha but managed to fall asleep soon after the plane took off from there to Nairobi. Feeling slightly disorientated and dehydrated I removed my jacket as I stood at the counter in the humid late afternoon air. The time was 4.30 pm and I had cleared immigration within 20 minutes and found the car hire representative waiting for me at arrivals. Jomo Kenyatta international airport was bustling with people and I was desperate to get out and get online to check the position of the tracking device. The fear that it may have been discovered or had stopped working was eating me alive and that coupled with the strange surroundings only added to my unease. Eventually I signed the forms and the young man smiled and spoke.

"Right Mr Green I will take you to the vehicle if you'll follow me please.."

We left the main airport building and walked down a pedestrian pathway near the drop off point. Desperate for a cigarette I pulled the box from my pocket and lit up as I checked my phone for service. It came as a relief to see a text message that read 'Welcome to Kenya' The air was warm and slightly humid and the African sun was starting to make its way down in the West. Soon enough we arrived at the car rental yard and made our way through a guarded gate. The orange Ford Ranger pickup was new and fitted with all terrain tyres. The young man de-activated the alarm and opened the vehicle before doing a spot check to make sure everything was in order. I stood there puffing on my cigarette impatiently as I waited.

"Well Mr Green" he said eventually as he handed me the keys "I wish you a pleasant stay in Kenya"

"Thanks very much.." I said as I crushed out the cigarette and put my bag on the back seat of the vehicle.

I climbed into the driver's seat of the pickup and immediately opened my laptop. The young man stopped to have a chat with the guard at the gate and I watched them as I waited for the computer to boot up. I tried, yet again to call Brandon's number but as expected, it went straight to voicemail. I attached my phone to the laptop with a USB cable and waited for the internet connection to show from the roaming service. *What if the device simply isn't working? What the hell will you do then, Green? You'll have come all this way for no reason!* This anxiety compounded by my fatigue stayed with me until the screen on the website for the tracking device cleared and I let out a sigh of relief when I saw the tiny flashing blue dot in the centre of the screen. I leant over to study the map to see the device was transmitting from a town by the name of Kutus. A quick google search revealed it was roughly 120 km to the North East of my location. I nodded as I recognised the name from the packet of coffee I had been given by Usmani.

"Makes sense.." I whispered to myself "He has his business there."

I turned the key in the ignition and typed the word 'Kutus' into the Satnav which was mounted on the dashboard. With the quickest route now showing on the screen I did another google search for accommodation in the town. There were a few options but I chose a hotel by the name of The White Horse Inn. Set in the hills surrounding the town, the place looked like it had been left in a time warp from the colonial era. Surrounded by thick Afro montane jungle on all sides, the quaint establishment had green lawns with croquet courses and there were images of waiters wearing crisp white uniforms and tasselled fez hats in a formal dining room. I called the number on the website which was immediately answered by what sounded like an elderly English man.

Although I was unable to tell the man the duration of my stay he took my booking and warned me to watch out for traffic in the town of Thika on the way. I thanked him and told him I was unsure of the exact time of my arrival but to expect me at some stage during the night. Finally I sat back in my seat and looked at my surroundings. The air had a golden tinge to it from the setting African sun and my body felt warm for the first time in a while. The feeling enveloped me and brought on a wave of fatigue but I quickly snapped out of it when I remembered Brandon and Sharon. *Get moving now, Green!* The powerful diesel engine roared into life as I tuned the ignition key and the guard saluted as he opened the gate. It took five minutes to leave the airport grounds where the Satnav instructed me to take a right. To my left, the massive city of Nairobi sat in haze of orange smog made more pronounced by the setting sun. I had read that the traffic in the city was horrendous so it came as a relief to find out I would be avoiding it completely. The drive North towards the A2 highway took me past the Karura urban forest on the very outskirts of the city until finally I reached the highway and turned right towards the town of Thika. Ahead of me in the fading light, the open green savannas of the Kenyan plains stretched out to the horizons. The road was good and I was finally able to gun the engine and reach a speed of 120 km per hour. Apart from the occasional shack on the side of the highway or donkey drawn cart, the road was clear and I sat back for the drive while I contemplated what lay ahead of me. Time was ticking against me and if Brandon and Sharon were still alive they would have been incarcerated for over 24 hours already. There was only one option for me and that was to find Usmani and get the information I needed. What happened after that was inconsequential but I was more than prepared to beat it out of him. The man and his family had been responsible for a world of hurt and I felt no sympathy for him at all. As to what I would do with him afterwards was still an unknown but I knew full well that Interpol would be more than happy to have a chat with him. *He's a monster, Green. Nothing short of a monster*. It was some 40 minutes later and the sun had set when I reached the industrial town of Thika. As I had been warned, the traffic slowed to crawl and the street were filled with pedestrians and hand trolleys filled with all manner of goods. The intersections were crowded and chaotic and the impatient truckers and motorists hooted constantly in frustration.

Thankfully the Satnav found a ring road which circumvented the centre of the city and I was finally able to gain some speed. I left the confines of the town some 20 minute later and drove off into the night heading North East. As I drove my mind was spinning with questions and fears of what I would face when I reached Usmani. *One thing in your favour is he will have absolutely no idea he has been followed. The element of surprise will be an advantage. What if he is armed? You hadn't thought of that.* These niggling thoughts and fears stayed with me for the next 30 minutes until I noticed the surrounding scenery change. The road began to twist and turn and climb steeply and I felt the air cool down noticeably. Gone were the shacks and truck stops on the side of the road and in the powerful lights of the truck I saw the surrounding vegetation change from dry savannah to evergreen mountain jungle. The road continued climbing and twisting through the hills until I reached the peak and finally I saw the lights of the small town of Kutus twinkling in the dark valley below. The road was good and wide and there was hardly any traffic and I made it down to the town in a matter of minutes. I pulled over at a service station and parked to take a look at the tracking device. It had not moved since I had left Nairobi and appeared to be in a nearby village by the name of Naru. I used the opportunity to try Brandon's phone one more time but the familiar voicemail message came up immediately. I was dog tired and my shoulder still ached deeply so I walked into the convenience store of the service station and bought a couple of bottles of mineral water and some paracetamol. I swallowed three of the tablets and lit a cigarette as I typed the word 'Naru' into the Satnav. The map showed the route which led through the centre of the town then left into the surrounding hills. The final part of the journey would be on a dirt road. I drummed my fingers on the steering wheel impatiently as I thought through the possibilities of what I might face when I arrived. *You're going to need a weapon of some kind, Green. Think and think fast!* A quick Google search for places to eat on the laptop revealed that I was very near a local sports club by the name of 'Clube Recreativo Portugues' or Portuguese Recreation Club. The establishment was known for its fine food and was open every night of the week.

I entered the name into the Satnav and headed off. The club was situated in a nearby industrial area and the wheels of the pickup truck crunched on the tarmac as I pulled into the car park. I walked into the front bar area to the surprise of a small group of locals who turned and looked up at me from their beers. The barman nodded and greeted me politely.

"Good evening sir, what can I get you?" he asked.

"Do you do takeaway food here?"

"Yes sir.." he said motioning towards the dining room through a side door "You can order in there."

I walked through into the brightly lit and expansive dining room. Apart from a small group of diners in the corner, the place was empty. The walls were emblazoned with large murals of various Portuguese football team emblems. Seated near the kitchen doors was an old black man wearing a waiter's uniform. He stood up as soon as he saw me and walked towards me with a heavy limp.

"Good evening sir" he said "Are you joining us for dinner?"

"Yes, please.." I replied as I eyed the tables.

"Table for one?"

"Yes.."

The old man politely told me to sit at any table and shuffled off to get a menu. The smells from the kitchen were good but I was far too stressed to feel hungry. Instead my eyes were scanning the cutlery on the table. All of the tables had been set with crisp white cotton table cloths and heavy steel cutlery which must have been made during the colonial era. As the old waiter limped away I quickly picked up a steak knife and surreptitiously slid it into my sock under my jeans.

I sat drumming my fingers on the table until the old man returned with the menu.

"On second thoughts" I said glancing at my watch "I have to leave. I might come back later"

The old man looked disappointed but nodded politely as I stood up. I walked back through bar and out into the car park with the blade firmly in my sock. Once again I typed the word 'Naru' into the Satnav and started the engine. The quaint town of Kutus consisted of a well planned series of wide streets lined with old colonial buildings. The hardware stores, builders merchants, and supermarkets were all closed by that time but the town was tidy and pleasant looking. I followed the route on the Satnav making a left turn at the grand old railway station with its brick arches and old English facade. The wide street was lined with huge Jacaranda trees and old fashioned houses as I left the town and headed towards the nearby hills. Eventually the street lights ended and the road began to deteriorate as I left the boundary of the town of Kutus. I glanced repeatedly at the screen of the laptop as I drove to check the flashing blue had not moved. Soon enough the tarmac ran out and I found myself driving on a heavily rutted dirt road of hard packed red soil. The road became steeper as I drove and there was not a soul in sight. In the rear view mirror the lights of Kutus grew more distant and a shroud of cool mountain mist enveloped the vehicle. The road continued up into the hills winding around sharp bends and travelling through thick impenetrable jungle forest. Eventually the road levelled out near a coffee plantation. Row after row of mature coffee bushes lined the road and up ahead I saw the lights of the small village of Naru. Consisting of a single street with a few general dealers and one busy bar, the village was tiny. I glanced at the crowd of people mingling around the entrance to the bar as I drove past. Loud, repetitive, distorted music blasted from a large single speaker placed near the door which revealed a sea of writhing humanity in the darkened interior. It was clear there was a copious amount of alcohol flowing and no one seemed bothered by me driving slowly past. I glanced at the screen to see I was very near the flashing blue dot of the tracking device. It appeared to be straight ahead but all I could see was darkness as the road continued up the mountain.

Soon enough I left the village and the road became steeper yet again. For a while it seemed the road led nowhere until eventually it levelled out once again and a tall concrete wall appeared out of the mist. The interior of the yard was lit by a series of lights on wooden masts. The property appeared to stretch up the hill surrounded on either side by thick jungle. At the rear was what appeared to be a double storey building with lights on each floor. It was as I drove closer that I finally saw the metal sign with the name of the business near the wall. The words 'Akus Trading, Deliveries' were faded on the rusted front of the sign but there was no doubt I had arrived at my destination. The screen of the laptop confirmed this by indicating the tracking device was now within a few hundred yards of where I was. The headlights of the vehicle shone straight ahead into the drifting mist as I pulled over, turned the lights off and parked. I opened the window and breathed in the cool mountain air as I stared at the dimly lit yard ahead of me. *What now, Green? That bastard is right there behind those walls. What now?* I pulled the pack of cigarettes from my pocket and lit one as I sat contemplating my next move. Through the blowing mist I could see that the only lights were coming from the security poles and the double storey building to the rear. *He must be there.* I climbed out of the vehicle and took a walk through the darkness towards the wall at the far left side of the yard. By the time I reached the wall my eyes had adjusted to the darkness and I noticed a large boulder that had been rolled up to the wall when the road had last been graded. I climbed up onto it and peered over the wall into the yard. The interior appeared deserted and I saw what appeared to be a packing shed half way up the property. There was a large concrete floor to the front of it with multiple rows of coffee drying racks at the front. The building was dark and appeared to be abandoned but it was from this vantage point that I finally had a clearer view of the building to the rear of the property. There were two vehicles parked to the left of the building and in the windows of the bottom floor I could see shadows of people moving behind the curtains. I stood there on the boulder studying the layout of the building. It appeared to be a home built in the style of an English country house. The style of the building work fitted in with the old colonial houses I had seen when leaving Kutus.

"Yes Mr Usmani..." I whispered to myself "Now I know where you are."

It was at that moment that I saw the swinging beam of a torch suddenly show from behind the packing shed. There was a security guard on patrol. I ducked slightly until I realised there was no way I would be seen where I was. Next I saw the arched front door on the ground floor of the house open. A large black man with a bald head stepped out and I watched as he made his way to the parked vehicles at the left of building. *Time to move Green!* I jumped down from my perch on the rock, landed on the slippery hard packed red soil and ran back to my own vehicle. Leaving the lights off, I started the engine and drove slowly up the road to the left of the yard until I had passed the boundary of the wall. I pulled over in a dark spot and spun around in my seat to watch. The vehicle that emerged from the yard appeared to be an old Mazda pickup truck with collapsed rear suspension. I watched as it trundled over the rough surface of the road blowing diesel fumes as it made its way back down the hill towards Naru village. I waited for the vehicle to disappear out of sight before starting the engine in my own truck once again. Certain there was no-one around, I switched on the lights to see that the rutted road I was on continued up the hill past the yard, more than likely to other coffee growing estates. I gunned the engine and spun the truck around on the rough road and began following the Mazda down the hill from a distance. *Just take a look Green. You never know.* From a distance I could see that the rough road had loosened the electrical wiring in the old pickup as the rear lights flickered constantly as it rattled down the hill. Soon enough the lights of Naru village appeared in the distance and I watched while keeping a good distance as the old pickup pulled up and parked outside the one and only bar. The big bald man I had seen leaving the house at the coffee packing factory got out of the vehicle and sauntered into the establishment. A group of locals who had congregated at the front door parted way for him as he walked. *Interesting. Who could he be?* I looked around to see the street was still totally abandoned. *Looks like the only action in town is right there. Why not pop in for a drink. Can't harm.* I drove slowly up the street and parked on the opposite side of the road from the old Mazda. Placing the laptop under the passenger seat I climbed out and activated the alarm. The punters crowded around the door to the bar were either too drunk to notice me or the music that blared out the single speaker nearby had drowned out the sound of my arrival.

It was only when I stepped up onto the concrete pavement to make my way inside that they saw me. The sight of a white man in Naru village was clearly something unusual as there was loud exclamations of surprise from the clearly drunk patrons both outside and inside. Nevertheless they parted way for me to walk inside and I did so with the pounding, distorted music grating in my ears. The interior of the bar was dully lit and smelt strongly of opaque beer and body odour. The grimy walls were covered with gaudy murals and adverts for local beers and spirits and there was a tatty looking pool table in the next room. The bar counter itself was a long brick and pine structure with wrought iron bars sticking out of it that ran up to the ceiling. The music inside was louder than it was outside and my arrival caused a similar reaction. Suddenly I was surrounded by a sea of black faces and wide bloodshot eyes. I walked casually up to the bar counter and ordered a quart bottle of Tusker lager. I had to shout to make my order heard. The barmaid opened the beer in front of me and then handed the bottle through the wrought iron bars. Gradually the banter in the bar returned as the punters became used to my presence. I took a deep drink from the bottle and turned to lean on the counter and take a look for the man I had seen in the pickup truck. He was nowhere to be seen and I would have recognised him immediately from his sheer size and bald head. As expected, it didn't take long before someone approached me.

"Jambo, bwana" said the skinny young man with dreadlocks. 'Hello, boss'

Clutching a beer bottle, the man was clearly drunk and tiny droplets of spittle flew from his mouth as he spoke over the racket of the music.

"How are you?" I replied.

"I am fine!" he shouted, clearly proud he had been the first to strike up a conversation with the strange white visitor.

"Buy me one beer please bwana!" he shouted.

"Maybe..." I shouted over the music "I am looking for a man. A big man who came in here a few minutes ago."

"Ahh.." said the man "Elijah. He is the owner of this place"

"Where is he?"

"Come, I will take you to his office..."

The young man motioned for me to follow him and staggered off towards the pool room next door. A bunch of tough looking men were busy playing a game and they stood to surprised attention upon seeing me. I nodded in greeting as the the young man informed them in Swahili that I wished to see Elijah. Clutching their pool cues they nodded grimly as they allowed us passage through the room and into a dark corridor at the rear. The smell of opaque beer was overpowering and in the storeroom at the far end of the corridor I saw the stacked crates of the potent brew. The young man stopped and knocked three times on a door to the left. Although I could not hear it, there must have been a response as he opened the door for me and motioned for me to step inside.

"This is Elijah, bwana.." he said.

The man I had seen leaving the house at Akus Trading was seated behind a large desk at the rear of the grubby looking room. His huge belly stuck out such that it was bulging over the pine surface of the desk. Even in the cool mountains of Kirinyaga County he was sweating profusely and beads of perspiration covered his huge cannonball like head. In front of him was a cellphone, an open bottle of Hankey Bannister whisky and a glass tumbler half filled with the same. The man looked tired and somewhat stressed but his face lit up instantly upon seeing me as I stepped into his office.

"How are you?" he said in a deep voice as he stood and offered his hand across the desk.

I nodded at the young man who had led me to the office and stepped in to shake hands with the man behind the desk.

"Fine, thank you.." I said as I walked forward "My name is John Garrard."

The man's giant hand enveloped mine in a limp sweaty grip and I saw that the whites of his bulbous eyes were cloudy and yellowed by years of alcohol abuse.

"I am Elijah Mwangi" he said "Welcome to my place.."

The big man motioned me to take a seat and he grunted loudly as he took his own.

"Do you like whisky Mr Garrard?" he asked inquisitively.

"I do partake from time to time.."

The man opened a nearby drawer and pulled out a glass tumbler identical to the one he was drinking from. He poured a triple shot of the brown liquid into it and pushed it across the desk towards me. I placed my beer on the desk in front of me and took the glass. The whisky smelt like petrol but I drank half of it down.

"Good, no?" said Elijah.

"Very good..." I replied.

"So Mr Garrard.." he said as he sat back and appraised me "What is a mzungu doing in Naru village on a misty night like this?"

I realised I would have to think on my feet. It was abundantly clear that my presence was highly unusual.

"I am a commodities trader from the UK" I said "I'm in Kirinyaga County looking for the finest Kenyan coffee beans. I heard there is a coffee trading company up here in Naru, but my journey took longer than expected and I guess I arrived a bit late."

Elijah Mwangi sat back in his chair and studied me with a half smile on his face. A bead of sweat ran down the side of his head and he wiped it with a damp hand.

"You are correct Mr Garrard" he said as he took another glug of whisky. "There is indeed a coffee trading company here in Naru. I am the manager of that company."

"Really?" I said "Looks like I found the right person in that case. Is your company Akus Trading by any chance?"

"Yes..." he replied, again with a half smile "That is correct."

I continued drinking and making small talk with the man for the next fifteen minutes as I enquired about the various grades and varieties of beans available. As we spoke I studied his behaviour and I became more and more convinced he had been warned of my arrival. The man shifted uncomfortably in his seat and began sweating even more than he had been when I arrived. His eyes constantly went to the cellphone that lay on the desk next to him. *He is desperate to make a call, Green. He's been warned that someone would be coming here. He's onto you, be very careful.* I waited while the man topped up his glass with a generous shot of the potent liquor before I asked the question I had been itching to ask.

"This company you manage, Mr Mwangi" I said quietly "I believe the owner is a man by the name of Akim Usmani?"

The big man coughed into his glass at the moment I said the name.

His bulbous eyes became even wider and his hand shook slightly as he placed the glass back on the desk.

"That is correct, Mr Garrard" he said "Why do you ask?"

"No reason in particular" I said "Just the information I have…"

I watched as the big man suddenly grabbed the cellphone from the desk and pocketed it. The chair scraped on the concrete floor as he stood up.

"Please excuse for a minute, Mr Garrard…" he said as he shuffled his enormous frame around the side of the desk "I need to visit the toilet."

The hairs on my neck stood up as the man walked past me and left the room. As he opened the door the distorted music filled the room and as he closed it I reached down to my sock to check the knife was still there. I quickly removed it and slipped it blade first up my right sleeve. *You might have got yourself into a spot of bother here, Green.* I turned the chair slightly so as not to sit with my back completely to the door. It turned out that I didn't have to wait long. It was only 20 seconds later that the door burst open and two of the tough looking men from the pool room piled into the room clutching their pool cues followed soon after by an alarmed looking Elijah Mwangi. Instantly the room was plunged into complete chaos with smashing bottles and multiple shouted threats. I leapt from the chair grabbing the still full beer bottle by the neck and spun around to face them. At the same time I removed the blade from my sleeve and held it up so it would be clearly seen. The speed of my move was clearly unexpected and appeared to unnerve the men.

"Right.." I hissed through gritted teeth "Who's first?"

The first man who had come through the door baulked instantly. His eyes flickered between the bottle and the knife in my hands until he decided the fight was not his. He threw the pool cue he was holding towards me and spun around to barge his way out of the room. The second man was a tad braver than his compatriot and lunged towards me swinging the pool cue wildly from side to side. But the man was drunk and I ducked and dodged the blows until the back of my legs hit the desk.

The heavy end of the pool cue struck my injured shoulder and sent a lightning bolt of white hot pain exploding through my midriff. But his forward motion had given me an opportunity with the beer bottle. Clutching it by the neck, I swung it around with great force. The base of the heavy dark brown bottle struck the side of the man's head and as it shattered it made a sound like a wave crashing into jagged rocks. His eyes rolled back in his head and he dropped to the floor with a badly lacerated ear. Next into the fray was Elijah Mwangi himself. He ran forward wide eyed, arms outstretched and roaring like a drunken berserker. His great weight was far too much for me to counter so I fell back onto the desk and rolled over backwards so I landed feet first on the concrete floor on the other side. The big man's momentum was too great for even him to stop and he tripped and fell heavily onto the top of the desk. As he did so he let out a winded gasp and his right hand slammed flat into the pine surface nearby. I brought the steak knife down as hard as I could and plunged it into his hand behind the knuckles of his first and second fingers. The blade travelled easily through his flesh and embedded itself an inch deep in the soft pine of the desk. Ishmael Mwangi let out a terrified high pitched wail which filled the room and drowned out the music from the bar. With the broken bottle still in hand, I leapt over the desk and ran for the door. Although there was no-one in the dark corridor, the scene in the pool room was one of panicked confusion. Crouched low, with the jagged glass of the broken bottle held out before me, I moved through the sea of black faces and made my way into the bar area. The volume of the music in there had ensured that the patrons were unaware of what had transpired in the other rooms. They turned in shock as they watched me barge through the crowds and sprint towards the exit. I burst through the door at full tilt and leapt onto the road beyond as I made for the pickup. A crowd of gawping and yelling onlookers were piling through the door of the bar as I jumped into the vehicle and turned the ignition key. The powerful engine roared as I spun the vehicle around on the dirt road sending up a spray of red mud and stones onto the shocked onlookers. The Ford Ranger bounced and skidded on the rutted and slippery surface of the dirt road as I left the small village of Naru and sped down the hill in the darkness towards the town of Kutus below. It had been a close shave and I knew I had screwed up badly and put my entire mission and perhaps the lives of Brandon and Sharon in jeopardy.

"Fuck!" I shouted as I gripped the steering wheel "You fucking idiot!"

There was no doubt that Elijah Mwangi had been warned that someone would likely arrive and start asking questions. Akim Usmani would be immediately alerted to my presence and would take some kind of defensive action. *But there's still the tracking device, Green. He wont know about it and right now that will probably be your only saving grace. Get out of here now and lie low for a while. You are filthy, stressed, and exhausted. Get to the hotel, set up the computer and watch the tracking device. There is nothing else you can do now.* My shoulder ached but my nerves had settled by the time I made it to the tree lined avenues of Kutus. I pulled over and typed the words 'White Horse Inn' into the Satnav. It turned out the hotel was located in the hills to the West of the town. My route took me down the main street, past the railway station, and up again into the mountains albeit this time on a tarred road. By the time I reached the turn off 20 minutes later, the lights of Kutus were once again twinkling below in my rear view mirror. The road down to the hotel wound its way through the hills crossing mountain streams and passing through thick Afro Montane jungle. The night was pitch black and at times it felt like the forest and the mist would swallow both me and the vehicle. Eventually I arrived at the hotel and parked in front of the reception in the small car park. I locked the vehicle and walked wearily into the reception carrying my bag. The interior was fully carpeted and had the old world look of an English hunting lodge. A crackling log fire burned in a huge protruding hearth opposite the polished reception area. I was greeted by an elderly black man in a suit.

"Good evening sir and welcome to The White Horse Inn" he said in a deep voice.

The check in procedure was quick and finally I was led down a carpeted stairway to the accommodation wing. The man opened the room and politely showed me the facilities. I tipped him with a $10.00 note which he took gratefully and left. The room was clean and spacious and decorated in floral décor from a bygone age. I opened a window and looked out to see an outside area complete with a swimming pool under a canopy of trees. Thick mist rolled in from the lush green gardens below and there was a definite chill in the air.

I swallowed another three paracetamol tablets which I washed down with bottled water from the mini bar. The WIFI code was on the laminated brochure I found on the bedside and I immediately set up the laptop on the bed. As I waited for it to boot up I tried calling Brandon's cellphone once again. The familiar voicemail message only infuriated me further. It had been well over 24 hours that they had been missing and I was starting to seriously fear for their lives. Either way I knew I would find out what had happened to them once and for all. The computer connected to the WIFI eventually and I was finally able to take a look at the status of the tracking device. The location had not changed and it remained in the grounds of Akus Trading just North of Naru village. *Good. We shall see what happens now.* I lay my head back on the pillows and stared at the ceiling deep in worry. I was dog tired and I felt grimy so I lifted my aching body and went for a long hot shower. The water in the hotel must have been from a mountain stream as there was a slight but not unpleasant smell of vegetation to it. I emerged from the steamy bathroom wearing nothing but towel and lay down once again on the bed next to the laptop. The hot water had caused me to feel drowsy and I lay there staring at the screen while my eyelids began to drop. I fought the fatigue as long as I could until eventually I drifted off into a deep dreamless sleep.

CHAPTER THIRTY NINE

Usmani

Akim Usmani fought to control his rage as he listened to Elijah Mwangi recount the sad tale of the encounter with the white man in Naru village earlier that night. The knock on the door of the double storey house had come at 12.15 am and Usmani had been soundly asleep upstairs at the time. He had found his manager drunk and sobbing on the doorstep while clutching his badly wounded hand which was wrapped in a dirty length of cloth. Almost immediately the whooshing tinnitus in his ears had returned along with a sense of extreme panic and fear. He stood there in deep concentration with his eyes closed as he asked his hapless manager a series of questions.

"What did he look like?"

"How tall was he?"

"What vehicle was he driving?"

"Was he alone?"

Akim Usmani nodded slowly as he heard the answers to these questions. He could smell the cheap whisky on Elijah's breath and this only infuriated him further. Once again he asked.

"What did he look like?"

"How old would you say he was?"

Eventually he was left with no doubt in his mind. The man who had been asking questions in Naru village was the same man who had visited him at the South London factory. The physical description matched him exactly. It was the same man he had pushed from the 17th floor of the tower block in Highbury. The man who was after him was Jason Green. The only other information Elijah had been able to give him was that the number plate on the orange Ford Ranger vehicle began with the letters 'ABG'

"Wait outside the front door for me Elijah" said Usmani quietly "I will be a few minutes."

"Yes sir.." came the solemn reply.

Akim Usmani made his way quickly up the stairs towards his bedroom. He packed his newly bought clothes and ablution kit in his new bag and took a final look around. Finally he picked up his briefcase and walked back downstairs. Elijah Mwangi was waiting for him outside the front door as instructed. Clutching his wounded hand and swaying from the alcohol, he cut a pathetic and forlorn figure in the dim light of the car port.

"Elijah.." said Usmani "You will say nothing to anyone about the events of tonight and the business must continue as normal. Am I understood?"

"Yes sir.." came the mumbled reply "Where are you going sir?"

This was the question that sent Akim Usmani over the edge. Carrying his luggage, he slowly walked up to Elijah and held his face inches away from his. The raging tinnitus had returned and his dark eyes burned with fury.

"You disturb me in the middle of the night!" he screamed "You come to my house drunk and wounded by a single man, whimpering and sobbing like a child! And you ask where I am going!"

"I'm very sorry sir!" cried Elijah mournfully.

Aim Usmani's tunic billowed as he spun away from the man and walked towards the parked Toyota Land Cruiser. He threw his bag in the back seat and climbed into the front placing his briefcase on the passenger seat next to him. The engine growled as he turned the ignition key and reversed out of the car port. Without another look at his hapless manager he drove down the hill past the packing sheds and out the front gate.

Within minutes he was speeding down the rough dirt road past Naru village and through the darkness down towards the town of Kutus below. Deep lines of stress and worry were carved into his forehead as he negotiated the twists and turns on the slippery dirt road. Akim Usmani felt as if he was under siege and his entire world was crumbling before him. He needed to get away and fast. Once he arrived in Kutus he drove into the centre of town slowly while keeping his eyes peeled for an orange Ford Ranger. Thankfully there was no sign of the vehicle and at that late hour the entire town was pretty much deserted. He left Kutus heading West on the main road towards The Aberdare National Park. An ethereal place of dense rainforests, lush green grasslands and hills cut through by rivers, ravines, and waterfalls. The drive there through the mountains would take him just over two hours. He glanced at the clock on the dashboard and saw it had just gone 1.45 am. His final destination was The Aberdare Club. A prestigious and expensive resort set in the mountains of the park, he had visited on many occasions in the past. Frequented mostly by wealthy tourists, the Club was a former colonial homestead and national heritage site with expansive views of the Aberdare Highlands which make up part of Kenya's Great Rift Valley. The African rain started falling, blackening the night further as he left the outskirts of Kutus and this combined with the winding road and rolling mist slowed his progress greatly. The events of the past 48 hours had taken their toll on him and he blinked and swallowed compulsively as he fought the dreadful tinnitus and negotiated the deadly twists and turns in the road. With his progress slowed by the weather it was just before 5.00 am and the sun was starting to rise in the East by the time Akim Usmani finally arrived at the gates of the Aberdare National Park. Feeling dehydrated and exhausted he pounded on the hooter impatiently as he attempted to rouse the wardens who manned the entrance to the park. Eventually a man emerged from the nearby warden huts and made his way over to the still locked gates. Wearing the khaki uniform and green jersey of a mountain ranger, the man rubbed the sleep from his eyes and approached the vehicle.

"Good morning" said Usmani as he opened the window "I'm sorry for waking you so early but I need to get to the Aberdare Club."

"No problem sir.." said the ranger with a yawn "I will open the gate for you now."

"One minute, my friend.." said Usmani "I need you to do me a favour."

"Yes?" said the ranger with a confused frown.

"There is a certain man from the UK. He is driving an orange Ford Ranger truck with the letters ABG on the license plate. We are having something of a business dispute and I was hoping to avoid him whilst I am on holiday here at Aberdare."

"Yes..." said the ranger with a slightly confused look on his face.

Akim Usmani pulled a $100 note from under his tunic and handed it to the ranger.

He knew full well that this was more than a ranger in the Kenyan Wildlife Service earned in an entire month in local Kenyan Shillings. The ranger stared at the banknote and frowned but his eyes lit up at the same time.

"I don't imagine this man will turn up here, but if he does, perhaps you would do me a great favour by calling me?" said Usmani with a smile.

The ranger thought about this request for a few second then shrugged his shoulder and took the note.

"Certainly sir. I will do that.." he said.

Akim Usmani reached into the centre console of the vehicle and pulled out a pen and paper. He quickly wrote down his details and handed the paper to the ranger. He then noted the ranger's name and went on to describe the man and the vehicle as best he could, to be sure.

"Thank you very much my friend.." he said "I am not expecting him, but in the event he does turn up, you call me immediately. Understood?"

"Yes sir.." said the ranger happily "No problem at all."

"I will double that when I leave, as a special thank you to you.."

The ranger stood to attention and saluted Usmani with a flourish.

"I wish you pleasant stay in The Aberdare National Park sir.." he said "I will call you immediately if I see the man you have told me about."

"Thank you.."

Akim Usmani drove the rough but scenic dirt road through the forests. The sun was rising steadily and had managed to burn through the thick moisture laden clouds to reveal a perfect blue sky above. The thick green foliage and prehistoric tree ferns that grew near the many gurgling mountain streams glistened with droplets of water from the previous night's rain and the air was sweet and cool. In the thick forests, troops of colobus and vervet monkeys were waking from their slumber and on more than a few occasions he saw families of warthogs with their litter of juveniles following in line as they ran through the jungle to their grazing grounds. The road wound and twisted and climbed in altitude until 30 minutes later it emerged onto a great highland plateau and the view opened up in front of him. The mountains of the Aberdare resembled Scotland in many ways, but here herds of waterbuck, cape buffalo, and eland shared the hills and valleys with lion, leopard and elephant. The hills and mountains rolled with steep forested ravines and picturesque moorlands with rocky peaks and cliff faces. Akim Usmani finally relaxed and felt he could breathe once again. From here it was only a 30 minute drive to the plush Aberdare Club with its green lawns, tennis courts, health spas, and manicured golf course. Here he would be free to lie low as long as necessary and finally get some much needed rest. It was 6.30 am when he finally pulled into the car park of the grand old stone building and parked the vehicle. The check in process took less than 15 minutes and finally he was shown to his luxury suite with views across the Aberdares and down into the Great Rift Valley.

He nodded sullenly as the porter opened the curtains and showed him the amenities and grudgingly handed him a 100 Shilling note. Finally he closed the thick ebony door and Akim Usmani placed his briefcase on the nearby side table and sank his weary bones into the warm and comforting memory foam mattress of the king size bed.

"Alshukr lilah.." he whispered as he closed his eyes. 'Thank God..'

CHAPTER FORTY

Green

I awoke at 6.30 am sharp and blinked at my surroundings in a state of confusion. Suddenly it all came back to me and I cursed myself for falling asleep. It was with a sense of panic that I sat up and touched the mouse pad on the laptop to check on the status of the tracking device in Usmani's briefcase. It came as no surprise to see it had moved but at the same time it was a relief to see it was still undiscovered. I rubbed my eyes and sat forward to study the screen. The flashing blue dot on the map showed Usmani had moved to a hotel in the nearby Aberdare National Park. I Googled the distance from Kutus to the location and saw that it was roughly 120 km through the mountains. *So Mr Usmani, you've run as expected. But where exactly have you run to?* A further Google search revealed that The Aberdare National Park was fairly remote and only had one entrance. This meant that anyone who entered would have to leave the same way. *Good. This'll make the job a lot easier.* It was only then that I realised how hungry I was. I opened a leather bound file from the side table and browsed the menu for room service. After ordering a full English breakfast I stood and walked over to the windows to open the curtains. The sun had burned through the clouds and mountain mist to reveal lush green gardens with overhanging flat top acacias and giant tree ferns. To the centre of the gardens was a perfectly blue swimming pool surrounded by layered beds of bright summer blooms. I dialled Brandon's number as I stood staring out the majestic beauty of the African highlands but once again it was to no avail. Dark clouds of worry and fear filled my mind as I counted the time since the pair had gone missing. It had been over 40 hours and I was beginning to have serious fears that Usmani had killed them. *Two young lives cut off in their prime. Wasted. You have to find out either way, Green. You have to find out!* Suddenly there was a knock on the door and I shook my head to bring myself back from my fears and worries.

"Come in.." I said out loud.

The food was wheeled in by a young waiter wearing a crisp white uniform with a purple fez hat.

I thanked him and sat down to eat after he left. When I was finished eating I took one of the knives from the breakfast service and placed it in my bag to replace the one I had lost in Elijah Mwangi's hand. There was a doorway leading out into a private outdoor area opposite the pool so I took a cup of coffee and the laptop out to sit down for a cigarette. A part of me felt as if I should have left already and rushed to him, but there was some common sense in what I was doing. *You need your strength, Green. If he is there, that confirms he has no idea about the tracking device. He feels he is in a safe space now so let him ensconce himself for now. It will work to your advantage when you suddenly arrive out of the blue.* The sun was bright and warm on my skin and the smoke from the cigarette drifted up in lazy tendrils as I sat there in the fresh crisp mountain air. After a hot shower I left the room and walked upstairs to the reception to check out of the hotel. I placed the open laptop on the passenger seat of the vehicle and typed the words 'Aberdare National Park' into the Satnav. The route showed up immediately. It would involve driving back down to Kutus and heading West through the Kenyan highlands for roughly two hours. I glanced at my watch to see it had just gone 8.30 am.

"Right..." I said quietly as I turned the key in the ignition "Let's do this."

The drive down the hills to the small town of Kutus took 20 minutes and I arrived to find it bustling with traffic and pedestrians. There was a noticeable change in temperature from the mountains to the town nestled in the valley and at one stage I broke into a slight sweat as I waited at a set of traffic lights. Thankfully the Satnav led me through the town without getting caught in the worst of the traffic and soon enough I escaped the town and was headed West on the highway through the hills towards The Aberdare National Park. What followed was what should have been one of the most spectacularly beautiful drives of my life as the road wound its way through the evergreen hills crossing bridges with fresh clear waterfalls and steep majestic ravines. Herds of waterbuck and zebra roamed the distant slopes never lifting their heads from their grazing. The sky above was a perfect blue and the granite rock outcrops glinted brightly in the warm sunshine. My mood, however, was dark and I pushed the vehicle dangerously fast around the bends in an effort to make time.

In my mind the vision of Akim Usmani lunging towards me and pushing me by the chest from the 17th floor on that freezing afternoon in North London played over and over again. My fears for the lives of Brandon and Sharon grew as the clock ticked away and I had to convince myself that this whole journey wasn't simply an exercise in futility. It was two and a half hours later when the Satnav announced I had arrived at my destination and I saw the green painted walls and thatched roof of the entrance to the Aberdare National Park up ahead. Here the tar ended and the rugged all terrain tyres of the Ford Ranger crunched the stones on the hard packed dirt road as I pulled up to the boom gates of the park. I took a look at the screen of the laptop and reached for the bottle of mineral water as I waited for the park ranger to arrive. A minute later I saw a man approaching from a nearby office. He carried a clipboard and wore the standard khaki uniform and dark green beret of a parks employee. He paused at the front of the vehicle and saluted me.

"Good morning sir, and welcome to Aberdare National Park" he said cheerfully as he approached the drivers window.

"Thank you" I replied.

The man proceeded to record the registration number of the vehicle and my time of arrival on his clipboard. I gave a false name and told him I was only visiting for day trip. Although the man seemed upbeat and pleasant there was something about his demeanour which bothered me slightly. My military training had taught me to pick up on certain gestures and behaviours that might suggest someone was hiding something. This feeling stayed with me as the man thanked me and proceeded to lift the heavy yellow pole of the boom gate.

"Enjoy your stay sir..." he said as I drove through the gate.

Ahead of me the forest thickened and the dirt road wound off to the right around a steep and heavily wooded ravine.

As I drove off I glanced in my rear view mirror to see the ranger had removed a cellphone from his pocket and was making a call.

CHAPTER FORTY ONE

Usmani

Akim Usmani was in a deep dreamless sleep when he was suddenly yanked from his slumber by the shrill and persistent ringing of the mobile phone on the side table. He sat bolt upright on the bed and blinked repeatedly as he studied the screen on the device. The caller's ID was not one he recognised but he could tell immediately it was from a local Kenyan number.

"Hello.." he said quietly as he answered it.

"Hello, bwana" said the man on the line "This is Robert, the ranger from the gate at Aberdare. We met this morning.."

"Yes Robert, what is it?"

"The man you spoke of is now here.."

"The orange Ford Ranger, you saw it?" said Usmani with growing alarm in his voice.

"Yes, he drove through here five minutes ago.."

"What of the number plate?"

"The number plate was ABG 3056, the man was alone and as you described.."

"Did the man say anything?" said Usmani "Did he ask any questions?"

"No, bwana" said the ranger "He did not.."

"Thank you, Robert" said Usmani quietly "I will pay you for this as promised.."

Akim Usmani lay down again on the luxurious bed and stared at the ceiling above. He closed his eyes and awaited the appalling rush of deafening tinnitus that he knew was coming. As it came he lifted his hands to his face and covered his eyes. Akim Usmani took a deep breath and let out a long and mournful wail of despair.

Outside the room, in the corridor, a cleaner heard this unnerving outburst and hurried on her way unsure of exactly what was transpiring in the room. With a feeling similar to that of a cornered animal, Akim Usmani stood up and looked out of the wide bay windows over the green hills of Africa and down towards the Rift Valley. On the bedside table was a glossy hotel brochure. He picked it up to see a map of the Aberdare National Park printed to the rear. The boundary of the park was clearly marked and it was immediately obvious that there was only one entrance and exit. But it was the Western boundary that interested him the most. The access road was remote and marked in red as only being accessible by 4x4 vehicles. The key at the bottom left of the map had a warning that this remote section of the park was dangerous with rough roads, steep hills, and dangerous sheer cliff faces. Experienced guides were advisable especially during the rainy season from November to February. An idea began to form in his mind as he stared at the map. He knew that he had the advantage of time and if he were to leave immediately he could extend that. The man who was pursuing him was alone and if there was to be a showdown it would make sense that it should be in a secluded part of the park. Any confrontation near or around the grounds of the Aberdare Club would attract a lot of unwanted attention. *No.* He thought. *I have the right vehicle. I will go now and await this persistent infidel bastard. Then we will see who comes out alive.*

CHAPTER FORTY TWO

Green

It was within five minutes of leaving the gate to the park that I noticed the flashing blue dot of the tracking device moving on the screen of the laptop. *You were right, Green. That ranger at the gate must have called him. He suspected you might be following. It's too much of a coincidence.* I stopped the vehicle in the dappled shade on a steep rocky slope and brought up the log of movements from the device. It had been stationary for 3 hours at The Aberdare Club and had only just started moving again. *No bother, Green. There's only one way in and out of here. You'll find him.* I headed off down the dirt road through the forest pushing the vehicle as fast as I possibly could. The heavy rains from the previous night had made the journey especially hazardous and on more than one occasion the front wheels skidded and lost purchase on the slippery hard packed red soil. Half sick with worry, I constantly saw the young faces of Brandon Stevens and Sharon Pennington in my mind. The forest was thick, so much so as to be impenetrable in places, and the many streams I crossed on low level concrete bridges were bursting at the seams with frothing white water from the previous night's rainfall. It was some 30 minutes later when I finally emerged from the clutches of the forest and drove out into the bright sunshine on the plateau. Finally I had a view from an elevated vantage point and the rolling green splendour of The Aberdares stretched off to the the Great Rift Valley on the horizon. Desperate for a cigarette and a stretch, I stopped the vehicle and climbed out. After the darkness of the forest, the warm African sun was like a soft woollen blanket and the air was cool and crisp. As I smoked I saw a herd of zebra grazing contently on a nearby slope. Overhead a fully grown Bateleur eagle soared effortlessly on the thermals in search of a field mouse or a rabbit. Its bright red face and grey and black wings stark against the perfectly blue sky. I closed my eyes as I smoked and let the warmth of the sun and soft whispering wind envelop me for a moment. My body ached and I was dog tired but there was no time to rest. *Get moving, Green. Now.* The sun had dried the road somewhat making the journey through the open plateau slightly easier.

I passed a number of open top safari vehicles with groups of grinning pale skinned, khaki clad tourists perched on bench seats with expensive cameras around their necks. It was clear from the branding on the sides of the vehicles they were all guests at the nearby Aberdare Club. This was where the tracking device had been stationed for 3 hours earlier. At the time I could see it was heading West towards the boundary of the park. It was 5 minutes later that I reached the peak of a hill and saw the manicured grounds of the prestigious Aberdare Club sprawled out below. In the distance I saw two white electric golf carts trundling over a fairway on their way to a distant green. The main hotel resembled an English country house and was fashioned from local rock, built by expert stone masons some hundred years previously. Blue woodsmoke rose from an old chimney in the main building from what I imagined would be a log fire in a grand reception area. I drove slowly down the hill until I reached the gate house. A security guard in navy blue uniform waved from an arched window and activated the heavily ornate electric gates which swung open slowly. The driveways were fashioned from cobbled stone and surrounding islands planted with giant prehistoric tree ferns and summer blooms. Groups of gardeners tended the flower beds sweating in the midday sun as they worked, while housekeeping staff pushed trolleys of crisp white linen down shaded walkways towards the accommodation wings on either side. The entire place reeked of colonial grandeur and opulence and I could completely understand why Akim Usmani had chosen the place to hide out. I stopped the vehicle in the sun near the entrance to take a look at the location of the tracking device on the laptop screen. By then it was nearing the Western boundary of the park and the road was faded on the screen indicating it was seldom used. I stared at my phone in the centre console of the vehicle. *Give it one more try, Green. You have to try.* As expected, there was no answer from Brandon and once again this sent a cold chill down my spine. I drove slowly around the back of the hotel and left through the same ornate gates through which I had entered. After taking a left at the dirt road, I drove alongside the golf course with its miniature lakes and rocky outcrops until I reached the boundary of the grounds of the Aberdare Club.

Ahead of me the peaks and valleys of The Aberdares rolled away towards the horizon in the West. I stopped the vehicle, lit a cigarette, and took a drink from the water bottle. By then the tracking device was showing it had indeed reached the far Western boundary of the park and appeared to be slowly moving North. The time was 2.00 pm and ahead of me was yet another journey into the unknown. I put the vehicle in first gear and stared ahead.

"Right.." I said to myself "Let's do this."

CHAPTER FORTY THREE

Usmani

Akim Usmani was starting to panic. He had been driving for a solid 3 hours since leaving the luxurious Aberdare Club. At first the road had been easily manageable but for the last hour it had deteriorated steadily until he had been forced to engage the 4 wheel drive. It was clear there had been little to no traffic on the road in a long time and the reason for that was becoming more and more apparent with every kilometre. Using the map on the brochure he had picked up in his room, he had ascertained that he had reached the far Westerly boundary of the park. Here the land dropped away to his left on a series of sheer cliff faces falling hundreds of metres and stretching out into the Rift Valley below. The road, if it could be called that, had become more of a rock strewn mountain track with terrifying and dizzying drops alongside it. Hugging the right hand side of the track in an effort to avoid the deadly drop, he persevered for another 15 minutes, scratching the paint work on the right hand side of the Land Cruiser on the bushes and branches that protruded from the mountainside. Although the air was cool, beads of sweat ran down his temples and his arms ached from gripping the steering wheel. It was then he noticed the small tree covered hill up ahead in the distance. It was somehow unusual and stuck out from the surrounding landscape appearing to be a landmark of sorts. He stopped the vehicle and picked up the brochure to see if it was featured on the map. It was only then that he realised how remote he was. The road he had been travelling for the past half hour had been marked as being dangerous on the map and had long been unused for this very reason. However, the unusual hill he could see up ahead was indeed marked on the map. An old and remote park ranger's camp by the name of Bayley's Lookout, it had long been abandoned and forgotten. Seeing it as a possible refuge, he engaged first gear and pushed on towards it. He arrived at the foot of the hill some 5 minutes later and stopped the engine. Directly ahead of him, a dead tree had fallen, effectively blocking the road. Even the thick steel bull bar mounted on the front of the vehicle would struggle to push it aside. Feeling somewhat trapped, Akim Usmani pulled the handbrake and climbed out of the vehicle.

To his left was a sheer drop over the cliff with various rocky ledges and stone crevices below. To his right the unusual tree covered hill rose up towering above him. It was then that he noticed the old track. Cleared many years beforehand, it had been originally cut into the side of the hill to allow vehicle access to the old ranger's camp above. Tall, waist high grass covered the track and it swayed in the soft warm breeze that blew in from the West. Akim Usmani began walking up the track and was surprised to see it was still in relatively good condition. Although it had long since been covered and sheltered by overhanging tree growth, the surface was in good smooth condition and this continued the further he climbed up the hill. Eventually he emerged from the undergrowth at a small flat clearing near the top of the hill. There were some scattered bricks and ruins of a old mountain outpost which had long since crumbled and fallen, but it was clear that there had once been prolonged human habitation there. The name of the old camp, Bayley's Lookout, was apt as from this elevated position there were wide-ranging views over the surrounding hills and the endless expanse of the Rift Valley below. More important was the fact that from this height there was a clear and unbroken view of the road he had just driven down. An idea began to form in Akim Usmani's mind as he stared at the treacherous road below. He realised then that from this elevated position he could lie low and watch the approach of any vehicle while remaining completely unseen. The fallen tree at the bottom of the hill would prevent any vehicle passing and the fact that there was a deadly sheer drop just to the left of the track provided an opportunity to eliminate his pursuer once and for all. Akim Usmani smiled as he realised the simplicity and sheer genius of the plan. The orange Ford Ranger would approach, its driver completely oblivious to the fact he was being watched from above. He would then arrive at the fallen tree at the bottom of the hill and would be unable to move any further. The driver would have no idea that the Land Cruiser would be parked half way up the tree covered hill and the long grass on the track would hide it from view completely. If timed correctly, he would race down the hill in the Land Cruiser and, using the heavy bull bar, would ram the Ford Ranger and the unsuspecting driver knocking both off the top of the cliff to a certain death below.

"Perfect.." he whispered to himself "Of course it'll work. It's Perfect"

Akim Usmani turned and ran back down the tree covered track to the parked Land Cruiser below. He started the engine and reversed carefully for a few metres until he was able to make the right turn up the hill on the track. Although the long grass blocked his view, the surface was smooth and it took less than a minute to get halfway up the shaded track. Once there, he performed a three point turn and positioned the powerful vehicle so it was now hidden in the long grass facing the bottom the hill. Next he ran back down to the bottom of the hill to inspect the area one final time. He walked to the edge of the cliff and looked down. Five metres below was a narrow stone ledge with scattered boulders and small shrubs. The ledge, although long, was only three metres wide and he gauged that if a vehicle was to tumble over from where he stood, it would instantly roll from the lower ledge to be completely destroyed by the precipitous and sheer drop below that. Satisfied, he walked back to the fallen tree and kicked at it with his right foot. The dead tree was solid, thick, and extremely heavy. It would require a chainsaw and a lot of effort to move it and he felt 100% certain that if the orange Ford Ranger did come, there was no way it would pass that point. Akim Usmani took one final look around to make sure everything was in place then made his way back up the hill through the long grass. He stopped to grab a water bottle from the vehicle then climbed the rest of the way up to the small clearing near the top. The warm African sun was starting to make its way down towards the horizon in the West as he sat down to watch and wait. It turned out that he didn't have to wait that long as within half an hour he saw the orange Ford Ranger as it came slowly around a bend on the mountain track in the distance. Akim Usmani lowered himself until he was lying on his stomach peering through the grass at the approaching vehicle.

"Right.." he whispered to himself "Keep coming. Keep coming.."

CHAPTER FORTY FOUR

Green

The sun was slowly setting over the Western boundary of The Aberdare National Park in the highlands of Kenya. The surrounding scenery had changed from green montane grasslands and hills to the more rocky and harsh environment of the high escarpment on the edge of the Rift Valley. To the left of where I drove, the landscape dropped away steeply on sheer cliffs with spectacular views that normally would have been breathtaking. Instead of admiring the view I had spent the last hour carefully guiding the vehicle as it lurched over the treacherous rocky track that had been cut at the very edge of the escarpment. It had been over an hour since I had been forced to engage the 4 wheel drive and since then it had been something of a white knuckle ride. On more than one occasion I had been overcome with vertigo at the sight of the perilous drop to the left of the passenger door but I had persevered by hugging the safety of the rugged mountainside to my right. I was exhausted and dehydrated but at the same time I was determined to catch up with Usmani and get the answers I needed. Even if Brandon and the girl were indeed dead, as I suspected they were, I knew deep down that I could never live with myself if I didn't at least try. Desperate for a break, I stopped the vehicle, pulled the handbrake and lit a cigarette. The clear sky above was starting to yellow as the sun made its way down towards the horizon to my left. The air was unusually still and the smoke drifted slowly away to my right. I turned to study the laptop screen for the 100th time and it came as a surprise to see that the flashing blue dot of the tracking device had come to stop not far from where I was. Looking ahead, all I could see was the rocky track as it wound its way around another bend at the edge of the escarpment. *He is close, Green. You are catching up. This is a good thing. Keep going.* It was five minutes later, as I rounded a particularly treacherous bend in the road that I saw the hill up ahead. Covered in mature trees and seemingly perched at the edge of the world, it appeared somehow unusual and out of place in the stark rocky landscape that I had found myself in. Nevertheless, I pressed on all the while acutely aware of the terrifying drop that lay only a few feet from the tyres on the left hand side of the truck. With my progress painfully slow, I eventually rounded yet another bend in the road and up ahead was the hill I had seen from before.

The glare of the setting sun obscured my vision somewhat as I drove but eventually I came upon a huge dead tree that fallen across the track effectively blocking the way forward. I frowned as I stared at the thick trunk of the tree. It was clear it had been long dead having fallen many years previously so it was definitely not a man made trap. *What now, Green?* But it was at that moment that I felt a cold chill run down my spine as I realised that all was not what it seemed. The sound came from my right and at first I had no idea what it was, but it grew louder and louder by the second. By the time I realised it was the roar of a powerful diesel engine, it was too late. In a split second, the ground around me rumbled violently and the Toyota Land Cruiser burst out of the long grass at the foot of the hill hurtling towards me almost airborne and at breakneck speed. There was literally no time to brace and the heavy steel bull bar at the front of the 3 tonne SUV slammed into the side of my own vehicle with unimaginable force. Suddenly my world was plunged into a chaotic and confusing mess of smashing glass and buckling, screeching metal as tyres howled on rock and my own vehicle was pounded towards the very edge of the cliff. The initial impact caused my head to slam into the sidewall of the interior of the Ford and my last memory was that of the deafening grinding and crashing of metal as the truck lurched towards the precipice. Then there was only darkness. I have no idea how long I was unconscious but I slowly came to with a high pitched ringing in my ears and a terrible pounding headache. There was a faint smell of scorched rubber in the air and I could hear a constant hissing sound from nearby. As much as I tried opening my eyes I could not do so, and my limbs felt as heavy as lead. Suddenly I heard the creaking of metal as the buckled driver's door was forced open and large powerful hands gripped me from under my arms. My head fell and slumped forwards as my body was dragged from the vehicle. Waves of nausea and darkness swept over me as my heels bumped over rocks and roots until the movement stopped.

"Fuck..." I heard the voice of Akim Usmani say in my right ear.

Suddenly the hands that held me from under my arms let go and I felt my body slam into the rock below. As I lay there I slowly became aware of a glowing yellow light in my eyes.

Finally I was able to open my eyes and I saw that the glow was from the setting sun on the horizon. I turned my head slightly to the right to see the smashed and buckled Ford Ranger sitting precariously at a 45 degree angle on the edge of the cliff. It was clear that the only thing that had prevented it from tumbling over the cliff edge was an old tree stump that had caught it under the engine bay. Even in my shocked, dreamlike state I realised it had been an incredibly lucky escape. I tried to lift my head but it felt heavy and sluggish. At that moment I saw Akim Usmani approaching. He appeared flustered and angry. He paused and stooped to pick up a boulder that lay on the edge of the cliff as he came. The rock was the size of a football and he grunted as he lifted it, holding at shoulder height as he approached. Finally my mind cleared as I realised what was actually happening. Akim Usmani had tried to drive me off the top of the cliff to a certain death below. His plan had almost worked but had been stopped by the tree stump that had caught the Ford and prevented it from going over. He had then pulled me from the truck and, realising I was still alive, was about to finish me off by smashing my skull in with the boulder he was carrying. I lay dead still with my eyes almost closed and watched as he approached. Sweat covered his face and there was a wild animal look in his dark eyes as he approached and stood at my feet. His grey tunic billowed in the soft breeze as he lifted the boulder and readied himself to slam it down on my head. At that moment I opened my eyes fully, brought my right foot up, hooked him behind the ankle of his left leg and pulled as hard as I could. The unexpected move caught him by surprise and the heavy boulder fell as the big man stumbled backwards. I watched as his eyes widened as he realised he had been caught unaware and had now lost his footing completely. A grimace of cold terror came over his face as he realised he was going to tumble over the edge of the cliff and there was absolutely nothing he could do about it. Frantically he began waving his arms in circles in an effort to regain his balance but it was too late. I watched as his body disappeared over the edge.

"Aaaahhyyiii!" came the unusually high pitched scream as he fell.

It was a full second later when there was a heavy, meaty thud and a gasp below. The last thing I heard was a long low moan as I passed out once again. I have no idea how long it was but I awoke as the sun was touching the horizon ahead of me.

All around me was dead silent apart from the whisper of the warm breeze that blew in from the West. My head was clearer and I brought my aching body up into the sitting position. To my right, the Ford Ranger still sat sideways at a 45 degree angle on the edge of the cliff. Behind that the Land Cruiser stood fully intact apart from the badly bucked bull bar at the front. The strange serenity of the scene was a stark juxtaposition to the noise, chaos and violence that had preceded it just minutes beforehand. I slowly got to my feet and edged cautiously towards the drop off at the cliff's edge. It was only then that I saw the narrow rock ledge 5 metres below which stretched out along the length of the cliff face. At just 3 metres wide I doubt that its width would have been sufficient to prevent the Ford from tumbling over, but it had been more more than enough to break Usmani's fall. As I peered down at him I saw him move and heard yet another groan. Even in the fading light I could see a large patch of blood on his tunic and it was clear he had broken at least one of his legs. I stepped back from the edge and made my way slowly down the top of the cliff past the two vehicles. It was some 30 metres further that I found the rock gulley that led down to the lower ledge. Carved smooth by millions of years of rainwater and animal hooves, it offered a safe way down to the ledge with the benefit of various tree branches as hand holds. Slowly and carefully I climbed down using old tree roots and blisters in the rock as foot holds. Eventually I made it down onto the ledge to see I was not the only one who had recently been there. The ledge was covered in various animal tracks, droppings, and old sun bleached bones. I walked back in the direction of Usmani who was lying on his side propped up on his left elbow. He looked up at me as I approached and I saw deep lines of pain etched into his face and the flesh under his eyes was blackened and shiny with perspiration. The evening was still and quiet and the cliffs and valley below were bathed in a warm golden glow. As I approached I saw that he had suffered a severe compound fracture to his lower right leg. His shin bone had snapped completely and a 4 inch section of shattered and bloodied bone had broken through the skin and was protruding from his leg at a 45 degree angle. A dark pool of blood was forming beneath the wound and his face and body were covered in a film of pale dust. Without saying a word, I walked up to within three metres from where he lay and sat down on a boulder facing him.

His dark eyes narrowed as he studied me and even through the obvious pain, a half smile formed on his lips. I took the packet of cigarettes out of my pocket and lit one as we stared at each other in grim silence. By then the sun had almost disappeared completely and Akim Usmani began to shiver. The evening was warm so I could only put it down to the extreme shock of his injuries. In the fading light I stood up and gathered a few handfuls of dry grass which I placed on the rock surface between us. I covered this with a bunch of small twigs and squatted as I lit the fire. The grass ignited immediately and the twigs began to crackle as they took the flames. Akim Usmani watched me silently as I moved around the ledge slowly and methodically collecting old branches and logs that had fallen over the years. Eventually I had gathered a pile large enough to feed the fire through the night if need be. The darkness had fallen and the only sound was of the chirping cicadas and the comforting crackle of the fire as I sat down once again on the boulder. The flames cast weird dancing shapes and ghostly shadows on the face of the granite cliff as the two of us stared at each other silently. Finally, after what seemed an age, he spoke.

"You came a long way, Mr Green.." he said calmly "Why?"

"You know why.." I said.

"But why do you place so much value on their lives?" he asked with the same half smile "You could have simply got on with your own. Why did it have to come to this?"

"I don't know..." I said quietly as I stared at the flickering flames "I guess I see things differently."

The big man paused and stared into the flames with the strange half smile still on his face. It was a full five minutes later when he spoke once again.

"So.." he said "What now?"

"Well.." I replied "I need to know. Are they alive or dead?"

"I see..." he said quietly.

I watched the man's face in the flickering light of the fire. It was as if he was weighing up his options and slowly coming to realise that there were very few of them left.

"It's over for you, Usmani" I said quietly "You know it is. It's not only the British police who will want to talk to you. It will be Interpol as well. You cannot move from here without my help. You would be wise to cooperate.."

The big man fell silent once again as he stared thoughtfully into the flames.

"When you came here.." he said eventually "Were you prepared to kill me?"

"Of course I was.." I said "Just as you were prepared to kill me, on more than one occasion."

"And now?"

I paused as I thought of an answer to his question and poked the embers of the fire with a stick.

"Now I don't care any more.." I said "All I want to know is if Sharon Pennington and Brandon Stevens are alive or dead."

It was at that very moment that I heard the thunder of animal footfalls and rabid panting on the top of the cliff above. The strange sound was accompanied by a surreal high pitched yelping and gurgling. Akim Usmani looked up with a confused and alarmed look on his face. Suddenly there was a rushing and thudding sound as the animals raced down the gully onto the ledge behind me. Some 30 metres ahead of where I sat, a group of the same animals had made their way down onto the ledge and were gathering in numbers in the shadows not far from where Usmani lay.

I smelt them before I saw them, and although I already knew what they were, I felt my stomach turning.

"What is it?" shouted Usmani "What are they?"

"Hyena.." I said calmly "Lots of them. They're here because they smelt the blood."

"Are they dangerous?" said Usmani with wide eyes and growing alarm in his voice.

"Very dangerous.." I replied as I calmly placed another log on the fire "Deadly in fact. But they will not come near us with this fire burning."

"Alshukr Lilah" he replied in whispered Arabic 'Thank God.'

More and more of the monstrous animals made their way down to the ledge and gathered in the shadows on either side of the fire. Driven mad by the scent of blood, their hideous shrieking and lunatic giggling filled the air along with the putrid stench of the rotten carrion that was their diet.

"They're alive damn you! The whore and that boy" shouted Usmani with real fear in his voice. "At least they were when I left them. I should have shot them but I didn't."

"Where?" I asked, my voice raised slightly above the cackling and yelping "Where are they?"

Akim Usmani went on to hurriedly tell me the full address and postcode of his secret safe house in Lower Holloway. He told me about the strong room he had built in the basement and even how he had left the two sitting there locked up with the light on. He told me how he had destroyed their cellphones and went on to confirm that escape would be impossible. One of the hyena behind me broke ranks, its sense of fear won over by the crazed blood lust. I turned to see it swaying nearby in the firelight with its huge snake like head lowered between powerful shoulders.

Its teeth were bared in a sickly grin and long strings of saliva hung from its quivering jaws. Its black eyes sparkled with excitement and animal greed. I picked up a burning log from the fire and tossed it towards the creature. It yelped in terror and leapt back into the seething pack behind. I turned back to Usmani and stared at him over the flames.

"How do I know you're not lying?" I said over the commotion. "You could have given me a false address. Why should I believe you? How can I trust you?"

"There is a briefcase under the passenger seat in my vehicle with over £60000.00 in cash in it. In the same briefcase are the title deeds for that house!" he shouted angrily.

"Ah yes.." I said "I know about your briefcase."

His voice was hoarse and filled with fear "Look at me! Why would I lie to you in a situation like this? I am telling you the truth!"

I stared into the man's eyes from where I sat and I knew then that he wasn't lying . Not four metres from where he lay, the seething mass of animals shrieked and yelped maniacally as they drew closer and closer. I pulled the pack of cigarettes from my pocket and lit one as I stared into the flames of the fire. Upon seeing this, Akim Usmani shook his head incredulously and smiled.

"Mr Green.." he said "Yours is a heart of stone.."

I took a long drag from the cigarette and let the smoke drift away in the soft breeze.

"That may be so, Mr Usmani" I said as I lifted my gaze from the fire and looked him in the eyes "But yours is a heart of darkness..."

With the cigarette between my lips I reached forward and lifted one of the bigger burning logs from the fire. As I stood up the cackle of hyena behind me shrieked and backed away. With my left foot I kicked the remaining embers of the fire towards the drop off leaving only a few red coals glowing on the rocks.

I turned around and began making my way back down the ledge towards the gulley.

"Bastard!! You fucking bastard!!" screamed Usmani from behind me "You said you weren't going to kill me!"

I stopped in my tracks and turned to look at the man with the burning log held up high in my right hand. His face was a mask of pure terror in the yellow glow of the flames.

"*I'm not* going to kill you.." I said.

Terrified of the flaming log I held, the slobbering and whining cackle of hyena backed away down the ledge until I reached the gulley. It took less than a minute to climb up to the top and it was as I approached the vehicles that I heard the first blood curdling scream from the ledge below. The Spotted Hyena is one of the filthiest and most hated animals in Africa. Well known for its foul stench and skittish, cowardly demeanour, its immensely powerful jaws are capable of crushing the spines and leg bones of fully grown Buffalo. With the flames of the fire on the ledge extinguished, it didn't take long for the braver of the animals to come forward and start worrying the injured man. Although he kicked and screamed at first, their gradual onslaught was relentless and cruel. Starting with his extremities, as one animal bit, so did another. Despite the kicking and screaming, the mindless attack continued. Stubby, bacteria covered fangs crunched through living bone, ripping, tearing and severing flesh until eventually there was a writhing, shaking mass of the snarling animals on top of him. In the morning, all that was left of Akim Usmani was a few shreds of blood stained cotton from his tunic that hung from the twigs of a nearby bush. On the rock surface of the ledge was a large sticky blood stain, but this soon dried up and curled in the hot African sun, eventually scattering on the warm breeze that blew in from the Great Rift Valley.

CHAPTER FORTY FIVE

Potters Bar, London, 10 days later.

A light sprinkling of snow fell on the soggy fields surrounding the gloomy industrial estate in Potters Bar, North London. Sitting next to me in the passenger seat of the vehicle, 24 year old Brandon Stevens fidgeted impatiently and drummed the fingers of his right hand on the plastic centre console. The sound annoyed me but I continued peering through the binoculars at the entrance of the building we had been sent to observe. It was our second day on this particular job and it was clear that the young man was still uncomfortable being cooped up for hours on end. It had only taken 20 minutes from the time of my phone call for the London Metropolitan Police to locate and free Brandon and Sharon. Apart from being extremely thirsty and ravenously hungry, they had emerged from their basement prison in Lower Holloway unscathed. Sharon Pennington had entered a local drug rehabilitation facility two days later and from all reports was doing very well. Ali Usmani had been initially charged with possession with intent to supply cocaine, and remanded in custody. But since the recordings of the goings on in the flat above the takeaway had come to light, there had been a long slew of new and far more serious charges laid against him. His lawyer had warned him in no uncertain terms that he would be facing a very lengthy prison sentence. After making the call to the police in London, it had taken me over an hour to topple the smashed Ford Ranger from the cliff top. I had to use a length of dried wood I found nearby to lever it over the tree stump had that had prevented it from falling in the first place. As expected, it dropped onto the ledge below then tumbled away only to burst into flames a hundred metres down. The Kenyan authorities never found the driver and it was eventually decided by the coroner that his body must have been eaten by wild animals. I immediately left the Aberdare National Park, eventually making it through the gate at 1.15 am that night. The sleepy looking female ranger who lifted the boom at the gate was overjoyed to receive a crisp $50.00 note as a tip. The sun had risen by the time I arrived in Nairobi and I immediately checked into a hotel at the airport to sleep and await the evening flight to London. I had destroyed the paperwork I had found in Akim Usmani's briefcase and bundled the cash, which amounted to £65,000.00 into my own bag. The money had been placed in a sealed box and delivered as an anonymous donation to the same drug rehabilitation centre that currently housed Sharon Pennington.

The donation had come as a surprise and even made the front page of the local newspaper. Slowly but surely, life had returned to normal in the frozen suburbs of North London.

"Is there any movement, Jason?" said Brandon eagerly "Can you see anything?"

I dropped the binoculars from my eyes and turned to look at the young man who sat in the passenger seat next to me.

"You need to learn to be patient, Brandon" I said "Especially in this job.."

THE END

Dear reader

I'm guessing if you are seeing this you have finished this book. If so I really hope you enjoyed it. I would like to ask you to please take a minute and leave me a review on Amazon and Goodreads.com. Your review really does help me to reach new readers. If you would like to read more Jason Green stories please check out my other titles. Finally, why not come and say hi on my Facebook page which you will find here: https://www.facebook.com/gordonwallisauthor . Thank you once again and rest assured, Jason Green will return.

Printed in Great Britain
by Amazon